C000129354

KILL OR

Part of an elite SEAL team, Mason takes on the dangerous jobs no one else wants to do – or can do. When he's on a mission, he's focused and dedicated. When he's not, he plays as hard as he fights.

Until he meets a woman he can't have but can't forget.

Software developer, Tesla lost her brother in combat and has no intention of getting close to someone else in the military. Determined to save other US soldiers from a similar fate, she's created a program that could save lives. But other countries know about the program, and they won't stop until they get it – and get her.

Time is running out... For her... For him... For them...

Books in This Series:

MASON

SEALs of Honor, Book 1

Dale Mayer

MASON: SEALS OF HONOR, BOOK 1
Dale Mayer
Valley Publishing

Copyright © 2016

ISBN-13: 978-1-928122-72-2

Praise for Dale Mayer

I love to read Dale Mayer's books... keeps me guessing.... I am getting good though trying to figure out who did it.... I am on my fourth book....

...Review left on Vampire in Deceit, book 4 of Family Blood Ties

Dale Mayer's work is always outstanding and Haunted by Death is no exception.

...Review from Haunted by Death, book 2 of the By Death Series

This is a GREAT series that you don't want to miss out on!

...Review from Broken Protocols Series

This is my favorite author I enjoy all her books and I can't wait for more... her books are easy to get into and I love the storyline

...Review from Dangerous Designs, book 1 of the Design Series

Dale Mayer is a gifted writer who now has me hooked as a new fan. She characters are complex and she shares her knowledge of energy work clearly and simply. Makes for fascinating reading...

...Review from Rare Find, book 6 of Psychic Visions Series

Don't underestimated Dale Mayer. Combination of JD Robb and Heather Graham. Paranormal suspense.........

...Review left on Maddy's Floor, book 3 of the Psychic Visions Series

Wow! I read a lot, and I can honestly say that there a few books that I have read that I will remember for years. This is one of those books. Thank you Dale for giving me the gift of this magnificent story. It was both heartbreaking and hopeful at the same time.

...Review left on Skin, book 1 of Broken and yet...Healing Series

Touched by Death is an outstanding novel by Dale Mayer. Unlike her usual novels that contain paranormal activity, this novel is sheer malevolent actions from ordinary humans.

...Review left on Touched by Death, book 1 of By Death Series

Dale's books are spellbinding in more ways than one. She has a unique way with words. Her characters are fun and funny and loving. I love the way the story flows. Her characters all have personality. She takes you from suspense to love, then fear love and eternal love.

...Review left on Second Chances, book 1 of Second Chances... at Love Series

CHAPTER 1

I T WAS A shitty day to die. And sure as hell wasn't on his damn list of things to do when he got up this morning.

But with a gun pointed right at him by an old asshole he'd been tracking, shit happened in its own time. Including in the jungles of Mexico.

Lieutenant Mason Callister slowly straightened, his hard gaze unwavering on his foe's face. "Daniel Hardesty. Nice to see you again."

The grin on Daniel's face was enough to make most men cringe. But Mason wasn't most men. And he cringed for no one.

Least of all this guy. Daniel had washed out during BUD/S training. Hell week had kicked his butt and had kept on washing his sorry ass all the way back home. The two men had been friends once. But not making it through the worst week of his life had left a bitter taste on Daniel's lips. He'd finished his time and walked away from the military first chance he had.

It happened that way for some people. Not everyone could handle failure. For some defeat ate a bitter corner into their psyche where it festered.

He'd never have thought that would be Daniel's path, but Hell week changed a man. For better or for worse. For Mason, it was that tilt of the hat that said he could handle anything. He'd already known it but having that added to his life achievements, well there'd been no feeling like it before or since.

Apparently, failing had an effect on Daniel for the same reason. He'd quit and gone to the other side – a mercenary for anyone with enough money to pay for his services.

"It's nice to see you too, Mason," Daniel said affably. "Especially as you're looking down the end of my gun."

With a slight nod of his head, Mason gave him the point. Not that anyone was keeping score. "And the woman? Where is she?"

Daniel's grin widened. "Not your problem."

"Maybe not, but she is going to be your problem."

"I see you know her." Daniel slapped a hand over his cheek and slowly rubbed the long red scratches visible between his fingers. "That damn woman is a pain in the ass. She deserves everything coming to her."

Mason's insides iced over. There were a lot of reasons for a woman to fight so hard she'd scarred Daniel – and none of them were good. "Being sold to the highest bidder? Really? She deserves to be kidnapped? Beaten?" There would be worse treatment for her too, both men had seen too much of it. Neither needed to bring it out in the open.

"She's developing new military tracking software. And she won't share it." Daniel shrugged. "So what does she expect?"

She expected her country to protect her. And Mason had no intention of failing. "So, she's alive?"

"So far. If she doesn't give over...well, you know how it is." Daniel tilted his head as if listening for something.

Mason did indeed. "Waiting for someone?" he asked casually.

"Not you. You're a dead man and she's going to be picked up in about…thirty minutes." He glanced down at the watch on his wrist.

That was just about enough time. Mason hoped.

A hawk cried, the large bird presumably circling overhead. Mason made as if to look up but kept an eye on Daniel. Sure enough Daniel looked up to search for the bird. He'd gotten slack. Cocky.

That was all the time Mason needed. He dove forward, grabbed Daniel's leg. The gun went off, but he'd lost his aim as he went down. Mason didn't waste any time, he took Daniel out in seconds. The unconscious man lolled beside him as Mason quickly gave a responding hawk call in return. Hawk, one of the men on his team, had taught them all how to imitate the powerful birdcall. Now they used it to signal between the six team members.

His men separated from the trees around them. Daniel never had a chance but he hadn't known it. Typical.

"We need to find her. We've got thirty minutes before she's to be picked up."

As silently as they moved out of the trees, they slid back into the forest. They knew Tesla Landers was here somewhere close by. And her time was running out.

Mason secured Daniel, resisting the urge to kill the bastard for hurting the woman, but he was too valuable to kill. They needed the intel he had.

Someone would swing by and pick him up in a few minutes.

Now for Tesla. She came first.

CHAPTER 2

TESLA LANDERS – HER friends had loved it when the car company started up, saying the two of them were well matched, both with innovative ideas, drive and a sleek look – glared at the dark plank wall in front of her. Tears threatened but she refused to let them drop. She had to stay strong. She had to believe she'd be rescued. That she had value to *both* sides in this war and not just the wrong one.

She had to trust.

Or else she was lost.

And staying strong wasn't an option – it was *everything*. Everyone had a breaking point. She refused to consider this was hers.

She would survive.

She closed her eyes and for the hundredth time in the last hour she let the litany of bolstering sayings ripple through her mind.

She could do this.

She would do this.

Every disaster had a silver lining.

The military looked after their own.

She was a valuable member of the team. Or would be if she could close the damn deal.

She couldn't help but worry that even for all those things,

they might not find her in time. The SEALs were good, but they weren't perfect. She clenched her jaw, willing the cry to stay hidden within. Her arms had been yanked and secured behind her, the pain so bad she'd bitten the inside of her cheek to hold back her sobs. She'd be damned if she'd let the assholes know they were hurting her. They looked like the kind of guys to get an extra jolly out of that.

Now, every breath she took, her ribs expanded and pulled on her shoulders. She knew she would move past the pain into a numb state eventually, but she wasn't there yet. She closed her eyes, wondering how the hell she'd gotten to this place in life. Right – because she wanted to save lives. Or rather, she didn't want more unnecessary lives lost like her brother's. He'd been stationed in Iraq when the truck he was riding in had driven over a land mine. No one had survived.

A techie since diapers, she'd been determined to find a way to track the weapons used against her countrymen and save more of the brave soldiers like Harry. To find the land mines before they were triggered. And that technology was what the enemy wanted. Why had she never really considered that if her software could save *her* people then other countries would want it to save theirs?

And how the hell had they known what she was working on? That bugged her. She'd been working as quietly as possible. The only answer was someone had sold her out. And damn it, that hurt. She knew her team. Loved them all. To think of someone doing such a thing broke her heart. Maybe they were desperate for money, but it could have been they were desperate to save someone instead. It was obvious the enemy wasn't planning on holding back and didn't care who they killed to get what they wanted. The only reason she was alive still was they wanted more from her. The software hadn't been completed. There were bugs still. A few things to pull together. But it was so damn close. They'd kill her once it was operational.

Therefore, they might as well kill her now.

Her team could finish the job for the Pentagon.

Maybe.

A tree branch rustled against the wall in front of her sending a heavy wave of pine scent into her nostrils. The shack was so old and rickety she figured a good shove and it would collapse. The sound came again.

She froze. Please don't let it be him again. The leader of this pack had terrified her. That he was as American as she was, made it all that much worse. She hated him. What he was doing. Why he was doing it. He'd been very voluble in what was happening and why. His explanations made her hurt that people like him existed. Poor humanity. It was doomed.

According to him, she was to be collected in an hour and taken to her new owner. Just putting collected and owner together in the same sentence with her name made her cringe. And that hour was well gone. She had no idea where the men were, but as she had nowhere to go, and couldn't move to begin with, she lay frozen on the bed. And waited for someone to help her.

And hoped she hadn't been forgotten or deemed not important.

A tiny drilling sound started right in front of her face. A minuscule hole opened up. She tried to shift back so her face wasn't in the firing line, but a tiny white light flashed in her eyes regardless. A startled exclamation sound followed with the light being immediately shut off.

She had nowhere to go. No place to hide.

The door opened quickly. She tried to sit up so she could see but could only lift her head and twist. The doorway was empty. Groaning, she flopped back down.

"Damn wind."

"Yeah, wind, that's me." A deep husky whisper floated over her head then suddenly hot breath rippled against her neck. She closed her eyes, shaking, waiting. Friend or foe?

A hand slapped over her mouth. Her eyes opened in shock, and she tried to pull back. Only the restraint holding her arms back released. Her mouth opened, a soundless cry escaped.

"Shh. Not a sound."

Her body shuddered in agony as her arms flopped forward.

"I'm here to rescue you," he whispered in low tones. "Do you understand?"

She shot him a fulminating look but gave a short clipped nod.

He slowly removed his hand. "Good. I'm going to sit you up and straighten your shoulders, so they will ease up faster. Ready?"

She nodded again. Like hell she was ready. Was anyone ever? But he gently helped her into a sitting position, her arms falling uselessly at her side.

He grabbed her shoulders and forcibly moved them back and forth, rotating them one at a time. Then he grabbed one arm and gave it a shake. He squeezed her hand. "Squeeze back."

She tried but the effort showed how little life was in her muscles.

"Harder," he snapped.

She glared at him. "I am."

"No talking."

Her gaze should have sharpened and should have been able to slice him to pieces, but then the pins and needles started, and it was all she could do to not scream. She tried to pull her arm back but he wouldn't let go, instead he gripped her hand stronger and roughly massaged her muscles. Like that was helping.

But surprisingly enough, it seemed to. Next time she managed to squeeze his hand when he clenched them again.

"Much better. Now the other one."

Knowing it was going to help, she willingly went through the process. As soon as she could feel and grip again, he stood up and tugged her to her feet. She swayed from the suddenness of the movement.

His gaze narrowed and he opened his mouth.

She shook her head and mouthed, "I'm fine."

He slipped to the doorway, peered outside. Then tugging her behind him, they raced to the cover of the trees. Once there, he slammed her against the trunk and covered her body with his back.

Squished but happy to be out of her restraints and away from the cabin, she wanted to keep going. He was talking in low tones to someone. Then without saying a word to her, he grabbed her hand and ran deeper into the woods. She had no choice but to follow.

Only he moved silently and she moved like an ox. Several times he turned and warned her to be quiet. Like she knew how to do that. The dry leaves crackled under foot, and there were bushes she had to constantly dodge.

And damn it, she was tired. Her legs were killing her. And she wore flats. Perfect for what she'd been doing and sucked big time for a panicked flight over rough terrain. She had no idea where she was. She'd been en route to Coronado, California yesterday. At least she thought it was yesterday but given she'd been drugged and her arm still hurt at the injection site, she could have been out for days. All she knew was that the sun was setting overhead, and she didn't recognize her surroundings. If they'd flown her somewhere she could be anywhere. That terrified her. What if she was across the world with no ID or passport?

Her rescuer slowed down and without warning shoved her behind him up against a tree again. Her back slammed against the scratchy bark. Thank God for the respite. She gasped for air. Her breath loud and raspy. She couldn't do anything about it, she had no fitness training for something like this. She did her gym time like everyone else, but running a couple of miles on a treadmill was a different story than running blindly through thick woods up a damn hill in panic for her life. And after a day of being tied up, her legs were actually trembling.

How could her rescuer see anything? The sky was overcast and even the moon was covered. She could barely see *him*. And he stood in front of her. She definitely couldn't see anything around them. Her clothes were black, but she knew her face had to glow in the dark – especially shining with sweat like it was.

Not a good day to shine.

Her droll humor helped her regain her sense of balance. She knew she could be off and running any second and needed to be ready. Unfortunately her body wanted to slide to the ground and collapse.

"Rest. We have two minutes then we're off again."

She didn't waste the energy nodding. Two minutes wasn't

enough time to catch her breath *and* respond.

She focused on her mental state instead. If that was strong the rest would follow. She hoped.

At the two-minute mark, she was hauled to her feet and dragged on another marathon through the bush. Why? If he'd been able to rescue her, why wasn't he able to get her picked up and shipped out to safety?

When he shoved her down behind a log, she knew she wasn't getting up again.

Not willingly. She closed her eyes and willed back the tears of exhaustion.

Damn.

"You okay?" That low deep note of concern had her opening her eyes and lying.

"I'm fine," she whispered.

His smile of appreciation warmed the coldness inside. When his grin widened, flashing his white teeth, and he whispered, "Good, let's go again," she groaned.

"Once more," he promised, helping her over the log they'd been hiding behind.

She didn't believe him but forced her legs to move. But instead of a run they stumbled. Instead of landing softly they came down hard, stilted. He reached out a hand. She put hers in it, loving the way his hand, fingers closed over hers as if he could impart some of his strength, his endurance to her.

Maybe she was gaining strength from him as her feet seemed to cooperate better, and she could pick up the pace. When they stopped the next time, she slid in a weak heap to the ground. She huddled up into a ball and closed her eyes.

When had she last hurt like this? Had she ever hurt so badly?

She didn't think so.

Her rescuer crouched beside her and said, "We're waiting for a pick up. Should be in ten minutes." His voiced deepened. "We're in Mexico and need to get across the border fast."

She lifted her face to his and wanted to cry. Mexico? Oh no. She wanted to be home. Away from this nightmare. Were they driving out? Flying out? By donkey? Maybe she didn't want to know. But whatever method she wanted to go now.

His finger stroked down the side of her cheek. "You're doing just fine."

"Doesn't feel like it. Feels like you ripped my ribs out and made me walk on them," she muttered.

His grin widened. "You got spunk. I like that."

She rolled her eyes. That was a first. She'd been called a lot of things but never spunky. Brainy, nerdy, geeky. Yeah, they had all been tossed at her head a time or two but not in a complimentary way. And never making her spine quiver at the banked emotion in a man's voice.

It was almost as if he was proud of her.

She wasn't proud of her. Good Lord she knew she'd start crying at the drop of a hat and look at the shit she'd gotten into. Her dad would have kicked her ass good for this mess. He wasn't going to be pleased when he found out. Then again, he wouldn't have anyone to blame for what happened to his only child and that would bring up his anger too.

She leaned her head back and closed her eyes. She had to survive. For his sake and hers. He'd already lost one child. He wouldn't survive losing another.

"No energy for spunk," she whispered, her throat so dry it hurt to talk.

A water bottle was shoved into her hand. Her eyes opened, lit up with greed.

She tilted it and took a long drink.

"Don't drink too much. It will be hard on your stomach," he warned.

Instantly she stopped but she didn't want to. She had to hand the bottle back before she drained the rest of it on him. As it was, the bottle was less than a third full. He must need some too. "Sorry, I should have left you more."

"There's enough. Rest now. You're almost safe."

He squeezed her shoulder before settling down beside her. She closed her eyes and rested. Only the sounds of the forest filtered inside her mind. The wind gently floated through, plucking a leaf here and there off a branch, picking up dead ones off the ground and tossing them in the air. But there were no birds. No squirrels. No wildlife.

Just her rescuer.

"What's your name?"

"Mason, ma'am."

She winced. "I'm Tesla."

"Nice to meet you, Tesla."

At the teasing quality in his voice, she tilted her head and opened her eyes. To find his head inches from her shoulder. In the faint moonlight she could see the thunderous frown, so at odds with his voice as he stared at her puffy shoulder. "What's this from?"

"They injected me with something," she whispered. "I think it was to knock me out, but whatever it was, my body didn't think much of it."

"It looks infected." He smoothed a gentle finger over the

puffy skin. She tried to hold back a gasp of pain, but he heard her. Of course he did. "It's hot."

She shrugged. "Of course."

"Not good." He rummaged around in his bag and pulled out some tiny tube of clear liquid and a small gauze. He cracked the tube and poured half the liquid on the wound. She gasped at the stinging pain. He poured the rest of the liquid on the gauze and placed it gently against the site. Somehow he had a medical tape in his hand and managed to wrap that around the gauze on her arm.

"That's all I can do out here," he said. "We'll get you looked at as soon as we land."

She nodded, staring in bemusement at the field dressing. Being an injection site, there wasn't much that the gauze was going to do to help the situation, but it would help keep it clean. She leaned back and closed her eyes.

But couldn't get comfortable.

"Isn't it time yet?"

"Another couple of minutes."

She shifted again. This was a horrible position. Everything ached. She couldn't wait for a hot bath.

He tugged her toward him, so she was leaning against his shoulder and hips. Instantly she felt at home. Comfortable. She closed her eyes and nodded off to sleep.

HE SHOULDN'T LET her sleep. Waking her up would take time. She'd be groggy. And needy. He couldn't afford either.

But she was exhausted. Injured. And needed rest. Where was the helicopter? They were one minute late. He could hear calls around him. His team on the lookout. But so far, nothing.

She moaned softly and shifted. He knew she had to hurt. Had to be sore as hell from being tied up for so long. The intel had been good and they'd moved fast. He had said she had spunk. In truth she had a lot more than that. Grit.

She'd done everything he'd asked of her. Without complaint. She'd only stopped when he'd stopped. He hadn't seen that quality in a civilian before.

He had to admire her for that. He knew very little backstory on her. Something about a brainy programmer who developed software intended to save lives in the field. He'd have done his best to save her without knowing that. But knowing that, he'd make damn sure she made it out alive. Anyone who worked and took the risks she had to save him and his fellowmen was worth everything he had to give. And then some.

A hawk call came from the left. Hawk signaling that a helicopter was coming. Good. That should be their ride.

This extraction was deadly. And the weakest link. They had to expose her to take her to safety. All sorts of hell could happen. He wanted none of them.

The second call came through. Confirmed.

Mason reached over and shook Tesla awake. She bolted upright and pivoted, her body in a defensive stance. *Whoa.* He stood up slowly, a hand out. "Easy. It's all right. The helicopter is here."

She blinked several times then slowly relaxed. Reaching up, she rubbed the sleep out of her eyes. Still silent, she nodded. He reached out a hand carefully, wanting to make sure she was awake and not ready to attack. He'd hate to hurt her at this point, yet he'd do what he had to do to get her on that helicopter the fastest and quietest way possible.

"Okay," she whispered. She blinked at him owlishly. "Which way?"

He grinned. "Damn, you're good stuff, you know that?"

She blinked at him again, this time in confusion. He wished they had time for more of this, but he could hear the wap wap wap sound of the helicopter. "Let's go."

Hooking his arm through hers, he walked her to the edge of the tree line where the clearing opened up. Large enough for the helicopter to come down. His men were hidden in position along the clearing. He counted them as he gazed around. Hawk. Shadow. Dane. Swede. With Cooper handling the chaos behind the scenes as he wasn't allowed back into the field until he'd passed his physical after being injured. Good. His team was accounted for.

He frowned.

Except there wasn't a captive. There should have been. He'd left Daniel for them to bring back. Where the hell was he?

The large black helicopter came in as quietly as a machine that size could. Before it had landed, Mason had Tesla bending low and racing to the open side. He picked her up and launched her inside then came up after her. In a smooth move they'd practiced hundreds of times before, the rest of the men boarded effortlessly and the helicopter lifted in a smooth movement. They were away.

CHAPTER 3

TESLA WATCHED THE trees disappear from view as the helicopter rose. She couldn't stop the panic from choking her. They were so damn close. Anything could happen yet. Please let us get out safely. *Please.*

"You're good now," Mason said at her side, leaning back to rest. He nodded at his team. "Nice and easy on my end."

"Yeah, wasn't sure it would go that smooth," Hawk said. "Daniel must have been lying."

"Daniel always lied," Dane added.

Mason nodded. "It's harder to deal with when it's one of our own turned traitor. Speaking of which, where is Daniel?"

The others shook their head. Baldly, Swede said, "He was gone."

"What?" Tesla watched Mason's gaze harden.

The group nodded. Swede said, "The ropes were there, cut."

"Shit. I should have killed him."

"It was the right move to keep him alive. We needed what information he had."

"I know that's how it's supposed to work," he said in frustration, "but I wanted to put him in the ground for what he'd put Tesla through, if nothing else."

"Still," Hawk said smoothly. "We need to know where Tesla

was being shipped off to, and who the purchaser was."

At the term purchaser, Tesla gasped then cried out, "Purchaser?"

Hawk winced. "Sorry, ma'am."

She nodded as a fine shudder moved over her skin. "It's okay. Daniel used the term buyer earlier. It just sounded different when you said it."

Hawk glanced over at her and smiled somewhat bashfully. "Still not something you need to dwell on. We've got you now."

"And thank you very much for that." She smiled warmly at him.

He grinned. "My pleasure."

"My thanks to all of you," she said, carefully looking at each man. "I do appreciate it. Wasn't sure how much longer I could stay in that position to be honest."

They all grinned. "We do understand."

She bet they did. She'd heard some things about the types of training these men went through, and her brother Harry had been a big fount of information. Filling her head with tales of what he and the others went through. He'd been so proud to be a part of his family. And that was what he and his men had been. Family. All family.

"Hey, are you Harry Landers' sister?"

She glanced over at the tall blond man who looked like a tree trunk. "Yes, I am. Was." She stumbled over the word. It was so damn hard to know her beloved brother was gone and wouldn't be back. She missed him so much. She'd instinctively avoided relationships with other men in dangerous careers because she'd suffered enough loss. But these men, one in particular had her rethinking that.

The men sat up straighter and studied her differently.

She knew they'd look at her in a new light. Harry had been a SEAL too. Hopefully her behavior wouldn't make them wince. That Harry, if he was looking down on her, would be proud.

There were few people in this world whose opinion mattered to her, but Harry's had been the big one. His team...possibly another. This couldn't, shouldn't be his team. But what did she know. It was a small select group. No, chances were they didn't *know* Harry, but they'd know *of* him.

MASON FELT THE blow to his stomach as if a torpedo had blown through. This was Harry's sister? They'd nicknamed him Dirty Harry after finding out the man could imitate Clint Eastwood and those old movies perfectly. Harry had been gone just over a year now. Mason had known him well, although he hadn't gone on any missions with him. But they'd been friends. Harry had spoken about his kid sister a lot. Affectionately, with respect and always admiration. She'd intrigued Mason. He'd always wondered about her. Always considered contacting her. But there was that unwritten rule about staying away from sisters.

So he had. After Harry's death he'd considered it again. Had even sent a card to her but hadn't heard back. Then that was to be expected. He was no one to her. Maybe a name but more than likely just one card in a sea of condolences. Back then, at the time of Harry's death, they'd all been in Iraq. They were leaving for a mission the next day but one superior took Harry with him on a trip to a different camp, needing to talk to him about a problem.

The truck had hit a land mine. They'd all died.

Losing one of their own was always hard. It had left them all at a loss.

"I'm pleased to meet you, Tesla. Harry spoke about you often."

She turned to stare at him. Those same blue eyes as her brother's made him wonder why he hadn't seen the resemblance in the first place. Because Harry was dark and she was light, as in ash blonde light. But now that he knew, he could see it in the eyes.

"You knew him too?" she asked softly.

He nodded. "We all did. He was one of us."

CHAPTER 4

S HE SAT BACK, not surprised. Then all SEALs had a camaraderie that was second to none. She might have gotten to know some of them if she'd lived closer to Harry. Had these ones been at his funeral? They might have been. She'd been so blind to everything but her grief. Now that she understood, she could see the resemblance in their faces. The same hard, dangerous look to them. Harry had sent her dozens of photos of men. Some here and many others. "I have a photo of you all. And more. From Harry."

They looked at her, gazes narrow, considering. She didn't know if they were worried about the type of photo she had. "He kept it with him all the time. You're all on a large boat, grinning."

"Ship," one of the darker haired men said in a pained voice. "It's called a ship."

She chuckled. "I know that. It used to bug Harry too. That's why I still say it."

The men's eyes widened in shock then the air warmed up noticeably as they laughed.

Harry had loved her teasing. It was one of the things she missed most. Teasing him and knowing it was part of the relationship. Part of the joy between them. They'd been so different. So much the same. God she missed him.

As she struggled to pull her painful memories back to the present, there was a flash of light and a huge explosion. A high pitch mechanical scream ripped through the helicopter. It listed sideways. She shrieked.

Mason grabbed her and held her close. Several of the men raced to the front of the injured machine.

She didn't have time to think what anyone was doing. Mason had his hand wrapped around her wrist like a vice on a board. But he was dragging her to the back, then he slammed something large and heavy against her chest.

"Hold this," he shouted at her.

Her arms closed instinctively around the harness. Before she could understand, he spun her around and was leading her to the side, locked tight against his chest. "Now if we get separated, pull this." And he stuck a cord in between her frozen fingers. "Ready?"

She stared panicked into his gaze. "For what," she screamed over the noise. "Are we going down?"

"Yes, the easy way." He dragged her to the side, the wind gusting into the helicopter. "We're going to jump. Hang on to me." He reached down and clipped their chest straps together. Outside the ground fell away to a valley way down there. Oh hell no.

"No. No." She shook her head. "No, it's not possible."

"Three, two, one..."

And he jumped, dragging her out of the machine.

Cold wind pricked her face, head and hands, but it was her endless scream that killed her throat. He finally grabbed her head by the hair and tugged it backwards. He lowered his head and sealed her mouth with a kiss.

She clung to him, her hands clutching his chest straps as her mouth soaked up his comfort. Whimpers escaped out of her throat.

It took her a long moment to realize her legs were wrapped around him, and she was kissing him back as much as he was kissing her.

If she had to be thrown out of a helicopter then it was a hell of a way to go.

She shuddered by the time he finally lifted his head.

"Better?" he asked, humor in his voice.

She heard it – barely. There was just enough volume in his voice to hear him over the wind streaming past her head. "As far as I can be…" she snapped. "Considering someone just threw me out of a helicopter."

"Would you prefer to have stayed inside?" he said against her ear. He moved his head to the side. And a whole different vista opened up. The other men in parachutes floated around them, apparently all safe. Thank heavens. Just then a huge blast split the skies behind them. A cry escaped as she watched pieces of the helicopter fly through the sky.

That was the first she realized only one big white parachute floated above their heads. She'd had no idea. Somehow she'd seen enough to know Mason would take care of her regardless of the danger to himself. Clipped together, their parachute was carrying twice the weight. So not good. Thankfully she was a lightweight. Still, she had one on her back so maybe that was a precaution only.

"Here we come," he warned. "We're going to come down hard and roll."

She had no chance to decipher what he was saying as the ground came up awfully fast. She screamed as they approached. A hard jolt, a series of tumbling rolls and he was on his feet, again stabilizing her as she struggled to sort out vertical from horizontal.

"Is it over?" she asked, hating the shakiness in her voice, clinging to him, desperate to have the world steady.

"It is." He was busy unclipping, unhooking and undoing straps and clasps until they were separated. And the parachute harnesses were on the ground. He quickly spun around and rolled up the parachute as it slowly floated to the ground behind them. The sky was black. Their new world a myriad of shadows. She crouched down wondering what the hell they were going to do from here? The cold was seeping through her. That wind on the way down had been biting. With no coat, she was damn near numb. She was dressed in only lightweight jeans, a t-shirt, with a light sweater over top.

Riding double, they'd landed ahead of the other men. She watched as the big white balloons floated down around them, the moonlight easily helping her to spot them. They were all several hundred yards away though. As if timed, they landed one by one and winked out of her sight. How could they find each other in this darkness?

The answer was so obvious she almost laughed. They were SEALs. They could do this blindfolded.

Mason turned to her, his pack already fully stuffed and reached out a hand. "We need to go."

"Go where?" She'd love to go somewhere, but...

"Anywhere but here." He helped her up. "I know you're tired, but whoever shot the helicopter down is looking for survivors."

That guaranteed her cooperation. She ran beside him, her feet shredded by the paper thin flat shoes that had long since done their job. She stumbled over a hillock and would have fallen if it wasn't for his arm. "Easy," he whispered.

She kicked off the broken threads covering her feet, realizing the remnants of her shoes were tripping her up more. Now barefoot, she ran.

At his side, her steps were long and free. With her eyes adjusting to the half light, she forged ahead, strong.

Mason ran beside her. He let out a weird half call. She glanced over at him. But there was no point in asking questions. They'd steal her breath and stop her rhythm. She hoped she didn't have to run all night, but she'd give it her best.

MASON COULDN'T QUITE hide the pride he felt as he watched this woman who'd survived so much, do what he commanded without question and still even after being tossed out of a helicopter, got up and kept on running. *Harry, where ever the hell you are man, you did good.*

But pride or not, there was no way in hell he should have kissed her. How completely unlike him and totally unprofessional. And if there was one thing in this world he knew for sure, he was a pro.

But there'd been something about her… There still was.

A hawk called to the left. He cut sideways and she never missed a step. He glanced down and realized she ran in bare feet. Her jeans were frayed and cut but she still ran.

He knew many men who would have given up before now.

Not Tesla. He didn't think she had any give in her.

Directing his path toward the tall stand of trees where Hawk was perched, he listened for the calls from the others as they moved to collect around Hawk. Time was of the essence. Not only did they have enemies on their ass, but he was pretty sure the pilot hadn't made it out alive.

Sliding into the shadows, he pulled Tesla around and into his arms. Against her ear he whispered, "We have to stay quiet and will be using our call signals. We don't want something unfriendly to come in."

She stiffened but true to from, she nodded. He let her lean back against the bark of the closest tree to catch her breath. The scratched and bleeding toes was something he couldn't do anything about right now. After they made camp, then he'd see to it.

The others came in, heads down, bodies low.

Mason counted them as they slid into home base. Swede, Shadow, Dane, Hawk. His mind automatically went to add Cooper but he was back at base.

Good. They were all here. He lifted an arm, and without giving any explanation to Tesla, moved forward at a steady pace deeper into the shadow of the trees. After a few moments, Hawk came up beside him and took the lead. The others fanned out around her. They'd do anything they could to keep her safe.

She was showing her mettle, a character that they could respect and admire, and then there was now the fact that she was Harry's sister. Interesting they hadn't been told that before. Had Harry told the others about the type of work his sister was involved in? The reason the unfriendlies were after her.

If they knew that, they'd worship at her feet.

That almost pissed him off. He had no reason to feel this way, but he couldn't stop feeling like those little feet should be his. And that was foolish. He'd planned to stop by and see her sometime in the future. To share stories of her brother, to get to know her. Harry had told him about her since forever. Half of the stories were obviously overstated, but...he looked at her as she ran, tiring but stalwart at his side...maybe not.

She'd been raised by a military man. A former SEAL himself, and although he'd wanted a second son, he'd gotten a daughter. And had raised her to be tough.

Mason had thought she was a marshmallow, but in the world of civilian women, she had showed herself amazingly well suited to handle life's bitchiest moments.

Shots fired through the darkness, splattering bark beside Tesla's head.

She let out a little shriek and collapsed to the ground.

Shit.

He dropped to her side, his hands already checking to see if she'd been hit. Please let her be okay. There was no blood that he could see.

"My head," she moaned. "Stinging."

He held a tiny flashlight up so he could see the damage. "Splinters from the tree."

"Hurts."

She was gasping for breath, but he wasn't sure if that was from the pain or the shock. Either way it was something she had to control. He plucked out the couple of larger splinters he could easily grab, then tugged her to her feet. "I can't do more right now. The others are small."

He watched her nod in understanding and try to regain control. She swiveled to look around for the others. But they'd melted into the shadows looking for the shooters.

"They are making it safe for us to proceed," he whispered.

Her eyes widened. She gave a clipped nod then in a low voice, she asked, "The pilot?"

He shook his head. He doubted anyone could have survived. The first explosion had ripped the cockpit apart. Mason had seen Hawk when the chaos happened but hadn't had a chance to confirm with him. But he wouldn't be with them now if there was a chance to save the pilot too. Not with those waiting on the ground watching, waiting to take out the survivors.

"Ready?" he asked.

He saw the despair in her eyes. Then the grit as determination lit their dark depths.

"That's my girl." He kissed her lightly again. As he pulled his head back, he heard the rustle behind him. "Hawk is here. Let's go."

Hawk took up the front position and led the way.

"How did you know it was him?" she muttered.

"I always know where my men are at all times. It's how we stay safe." It might be, but she was a distraction he could ill afford. What was wrong with him? He couldn't stop kissing her.

"And never leave any man behind, I believe."

"No man is left behind," he confirmed, feeling the vow he'd taken deep inside.

And in this case, no woman either.

CHAPTER 5

S HE HAD TO stop. Except she refused to be the first one. And that was damn stupid. She wasn't trained for this. They were. She should have stopped a long time ago. For the tenth time in the same number of minutes she stumbled. Mason once again caught her. Without missing a stride he swooped down and picked her up, still moving at top speed, but now with her in his arms.

"I can run," she protested.

"No, you're done."

She didn't argue. She was too damn happy to not be trying to power along at his side. He was right. She was done. And she hurt enough already that the jostling of being carried was making it worse.

Then he said it. "You were slowing us down."

"What?" she exclaimed in hoarse outrage. "I was not."

But she had been, she realized. They were moving faster. The men had picked up the speed now that they weren't maintaining the pace she'd set.

"Sorry," she muttered against his neck.

He squeezed her close. "You're doing wonderful. Just keep it up."

She closed her eyes, letting her body relax, adjust to the

swaying movement as he ran. Comfortable as she could be, warm against his chest and so very tired she dozed lightly.

"She's held up well," said a deep voice beside her.

She thought that was Swede but was too comfortable to care enough to open her eyes and look.

"She has."

"Hard to believe she's Harry's sister."

"But appropriate."

"Same spine." The man gave a half snort. "Let me know, huh?"

Silence.

In her drowsy state she couldn't quite follow the conversation. It was more a drifting noise in the background. Words flowing but not making any sense...

"Nothing to let you know about," Mason said in low tones.

The other man laughed. "Right. You are in denial."

"No denial here."

"Good, then when you make up your mind about her. Let me know. If you're not keeping her, she's available."

"No, she's not."

The same laughter.

A new voice joked, "If you're not keeping her then there are more of us interested."

Mason snapped, "Let's keep our eye on the job."

"Sure. The job. The damned prettiest job I've seen in a long time."

Yet another voice popped in. "And who knows how this would have worked out if someone else had rescued her from the shack."

Muffled laughter filled the air.

She finally understood where this conversation was going. With that in mind, she made an audible groan and opened her eyes, giving the men lots of warning.

She was no prize.

And there was no way Mason would be keeping her.

Neither would any of these other men.

She wasn't a possession. And she wasn't a kept woman.

She was a big fan of these men though.

Especially the one who held her close to his chest.

"HOW ARE YOU feeling?" Mason asked in between dodging the trees. He'd kick the others if they woke her. She needed her rest. He also hoped she'd missed the conversation if she'd just woken up. Not that she'd have understood it in the first place.

It was an old joke. But one he didn't want to have to explain.

The men were all jesters. And he was one of them.

He slowed his pace as the others motioned they were stopping.

"What have you found?" he asked in a low voice.

"An old camp on the left, likely a hunting camp."

"On the map?"

"No."

"Good. Let's see what we've got."

Silently, the others did a quick search before returning as silently as they'd come. Mason held Tesla on her feet, steadying her as they waited. They'd be fine outside overnight, but she'd do better in a shelter. What they couldn't do was leave a trace of their passing. If there was a camp down there it was likely it was more of a shack. But if the weather held, it would do nicely.

Small, it would be easy enough to set up a perimeter watch, and taking turns, they'd be able to rest.

At the all clear signal, he helped Tesla to the small cabin. Inside were several old chairs and a small table. She sat down while he unloaded the packs. "First things first…"

"Tea?" she asked hopefully.

"No, but nice try. We'll put that on the list though."

"So what's first," she said in a lost voice. She slid her arms forward on the table and laid her head down. Only to bolt upright with a small cry of pain.

"That's the first priority." Mason pulled out his field pack. A quick search of the cabin showed a lantern sitting on a shelf. He pondered the risk of lighting it. Optioning for the safer route, he opened a small flashlight and had her hold it while he picked the slivers out of her scalp. She stared at him the whole time, her eyes huge.

After the first stifled cry she hadn't said a word. He hurt for her. Too often the small injuries were the worst and as he pulled splinter after splinter out, he was the one wincing. Damn. She was getting under his skin. In a big way. Just a couple more…and finally he was done.

"There, it's all good."

She stared deep into his gaze as if waiting for him to say something to contradict his last statement.

"That was the last one."

She closed her eyes with relief and gave a curt nod. Within seconds she'd slumped to the table, her head resting on her folded arms.

And slept.

Mason cleaned up then stood and quickly made her a makeshift bed. After picking her up and laying her down on it, he covered her up with his coat.

Standing back up, he stared at her. What the hell was he going to do with her?

"Damn," he muttered, unable to pull himself away.

She whimpered in her sleep. He knelt down and placed a hand on her shoulders. "Easy, Tesla. You're safe now."

She stilled and dropped deeper into a dreamless state.

Her color was pale, the small pinprick wounds on the side of her face showing stark against her white skin. Shivers still wracked her frame as she slept. He needed to clean her feet. Maybe he could do so while she slept. He didn't have much to work with, but he got busy doing the little he could.

She slept through it.

Good.

If she could get some rest, tomorrow would be that much easier.

They were searching for another pickup location. They needed to get her out before they were found. The area was heavily wooded. They weren't out of danger and would need to be on watch overnight. And as evidenced by what happened on the helicopter, the enemy wasn't going to let her go so easily.

CHAPTER 6

S HE'D SPENT WAY too much time sleeping and recovering during this nightmare. Tesla lay quietly in the early morning dawn. She knew they'd be up soon and on the run. Unfortunately. She was exhausted. Just the thought of getting up was enough to make her body feel like lead. Quitting wasn't an option. She had to hold up. Harry would expect nothing less. Neither would her father. It didn't matter that any other person would understand weakness in this situation because she knew her brother and father wouldn't show any.

Harry would more than her father. Her father was a hard ass. Her mother had died a decade ago now. She and Harry had become closer after the loss whereas her father had become more distant. Colder. As if it was his way to avoid being hurt again. Weakness was to be avoided at all costs. Considering he was a former SEAL and weakness wasn't in their vocabulary, she could understand. That she was here in this situation was not something anyone could prepare her for though. She had no training for something like this.

"Are you going to wake her," Swede asked in a low voice. "We've got ten minutes."

"I was trying to give her as much time as I can."

"Understood."

Silence.

"Damn," Mason growled. "I'll wake her now."

"Don't bother," Tesla said, rolling over and sitting up. The movement caused her to suck in her breath and shudder as muscles screamed at her after stiffening overnight. It took a long moment to suck it up and speak again, "I'm awake."

"Good."

She stared at the four huge calendar model males. Talk about gorgeous... They stared back at her in silence. Thankfully without having a clue as to what was crossing her mind. She sighed. "I guess that means time to go?"

"You get a few minutes to eat."

She brightened. "Food would be good." She struggled to her feet until she tried to put weight on her puffy soles. She collapsed instantly, tumbling back onto the makeshift bed. "Shit."

Instantly Mason was at her side. "Your feet?"

"Yeah. I'm fine. It was just the shock," she muttered. *Please let it be just the shock.* She had to be able to walk.

"Lie still for a moment. I cleaned them last night but the light was bad, so I need to take another look now."

"You cleaned them?" she asked in astonishment. "Really?"

"Yes, after you fell asleep."

Oh shit. Chagrined to realize a man could actually wash her feet while she slept was a little unsettling. She sat up as he took a careful look at first one then the second. He pulled out a thick cream and coated the soles of both liberally then slowly eased two thick pairs of socks over her raw skin. She stared, open mouthed as he finished.

"These should help. Now try to stand."

With his help she gained her feet. Thankfully the socks offered a thick cushion for her weight. She smiled gratefully. "Thank you. I was worried about how I was going to be able to walk today."

"When those socks run through," he said, "the guys each have spares with them, too."

It took her a moment to realize that meant she was wearing his spare socks. "Thank you."

He gave her a slow smile that zinged to her heart. "No problem."

Giving her space, he stepped back and let her hobble her way to the table. She stopped just before and looked around hopefully. "I don't suppose you found a lovely bathroom with a proper toilet anywhere close by?"

"Not a one. No bubble baths or bottles of wine either."

"Damn. Must remember to send a complaint to the manager," she said cheerfully. "So I have to go to the bathroom, outside?"

Mason stepped up. "Outside around the back of the cabin. And I'll be standing watch."

"Of course you will." She groaned comically. "Show me where, please."

She followed him around the small bushes at the back of the cabin. "Yep, definitely need to write the establishment," she said.

"Glad you're finding something to laugh about." Mason gave her a small nudge. "Go on. I'll keep my back turned."

"Great. Well, let's see if I can do this quickly."

It was awkward and uncomfortable given the sore legs and puffy feet. When done, she stood up, rearranged her clothing and called out, "I'm done."

"Good. Inside. You get a few minutes then we need to

leave."

Of course they did. Would this never end? Inside she washed, then scarfed the few rations the men had shared and drank a half bottle of water. Resolute, she turned to face them, all waiting and standing in various relaxed positions that completely belied their inner guard that was always on.

"Okay," she said. "What's next?"

"There's a small town a couple of miles away. Hawk has gone to check it out. We'll round up a vehicle and arrange for you to be picked up."

"Sounds good." In fact, only a couple of miles away sounded lovely. She could do that. She hoped.

In silence, they filed out in a single line, with Tesla in the middle. She breathed in the fresh air now that she had a moment to look around. There was a boggy spot on the left hand side. She heard ducks flying overhead and song birds chirping in the tree. The sun was just breaking over the crest.

"Are we still in Mexico?" she asked in wonder. The trees offered a mix of smells that lifted and changed with the breeze.

It was surprisingly beautiful.

In any other circumstances, she'd love to spend some time here.

Then again, she'd loved to spend time in lots of places. She worked long and hard yet spent little on herself. She needed time off. Relax a little. These last few days, she'd come close to losing everything. She didn't think anything the group that kidnapped her offered was going to be anything she'd like to accept. Death was not just a possibility, but rather a probability. And she still didn't know which group it was. Not that it mattered. They were all bad news.

And these men had saved her from that.

There was a loud disturbance from a cluster of brush on the right. Instinctively she dropped to the ground. When no one reassured her it was all right to stand up again, she realized her instincts were correct.

"Yes," Mason said. "According to the GPS, we're almost at the border. Let's move."

Crowded beside her, Mason kept a hand on her shoulder. She watched as he searched the area visually. He checked his watch – if that was a watch given that it held more dials and switches than a watch could possibly hold. Catching her glance, he smiled reassuringly at her.

"We're just checking."

There were a couple of short bursts of pops. She frowned. "Was that–"

"We've got this."

She believed him.

"Shit," he murmured. "Stay down." And he flattened onto the ground beside her, placed a finger to her lips.

Wordlessly she asked if they were no longer alone.

But his narrowed gaze never changed.

She closed her eyes. *Please let this be over.*

"Well, well. What do we have here?" A rough chuckle yelled in her ears. "Must be my lucky day."

Oh crap. Her gaze flew open to see a white male dressed in camouflage gear staring down at them. A rifle pointed at the two of them. A rifle. Interesting choice. Her mind rushed in circles looking at options.

"Get up…slowly."

"Hello?" she scrambled to her feet. "My goodness. Have I

done something wrong?" she asked in what she hoped was an innocent voice.

"Easy, Tesla," Mason said in a hard voice. "He knows exactly who we are."

"Of course I do." The gunman smiled. "And you have something that belongs to me."

"Belongs to you?" Tesla said in confusion.

"Don't be stupid," he snarled. "Walk over here beside me."

She glanced at Mason but he wasn't helping. Instead, he looked to be more bored and irritated than worried. As if trying to decide which course of action to take. She'd do what she could to give him that time. She shrugged and said, "No."

The enemy's eyebrows shot up. "What did you say, bitch?"

"I said, no. I'm not going to walk over to you," she said defiantly and waited for his next move. They needed her alive – at least she was gambling on that point.

"Do you think I give a shit what you do? I'd as soon as shoot you where you stand."

She raised her eyebrows. "I hardly think that's what your bosses have in mind."

The rifle was raised in her direction. She swallowed hard, then straightened her back. "Then shoot me if I have no value to you. What's the point of forcing me to walk anymore?"

"Shut up. You're coming with me. He, on the other hand, is a dead man."

The rifle swept toward Mason.

"No, stop," she cried out, stepping in front of Mason. He'd already saved her life several times. She couldn't stand by and have him make the ultimate sacrifice.

"Tesla," Mason growled. "Move back."

"No," she snapped. "This coward would shoot you, unarmed." She glared at the man holding the gun. "Have you no honor?"

The weapon fired harmlessly in the air. "Do you think I'm joking?"

"No. Not at all." She stepped forward. "But you will let him go or I won't cooperate."

"I don't give a fuck if you cooperate or not."

Behind him, she saw Hawk coming through the long grass. Why didn't he shoot? It would be all over. She had to keep the gunman distracted.

"Move or I'll shoot him through you." He snarled. "I can carry you for the few miles required. I know how to shoot you so that you are in great pain but not in any life threatening danger."

Her mouth opened. She didn't know what to say.

He laughed. "You stupid bit–"

The knife came out from behind and sliced deep. The enemy gurgled quietly as he was lowered to the ground – already dead.

Tesla gasped as Mason pulled her away and behind him.

With Hawk in the lead, they raced to the cover of the trees.

There Hawk explained they'd found two more in the bushes. Both taken care of. They were concerned there was a fourth, but they hadn't located him. The rest of Mason's team were on route to the village, hoping to flush out the enemy that could be there ahead of them.

Waiting for their own men to arrive first.

With time against them and knowing the fourth man was on the trail, Mason pushed Tesla harder than he had yet. By the time they reached the hill overlooking the small town, she dropped to the ground and held her ribs as she tried to catch her breath. Her feet were killing her. Whatever slight joy she'd experienced upon first standing was gone a long time ago. She studied the bloody remnant of the socks and realized they were useless now too. Her jeans had several new tears in the legs as well. And her shirt, well that was damn near destroyed. Her light sweater was grimy and hung in tatters.

Crap.

She tried to focus on the mundane issue of clothes. Anything to forget the image of the man's blood gushing from his neck or the limp way he went down in Hawk's arms.

Uncontrollable shivers ripped down her body. She wrapped her arms around her knees and hung on, waiting, hoping for the shock to ease back. God, that poor man.

She knew he would have done the same thing to her men if he'd had the chance. And would have shot her just to get at Mason. This really was happening. They were really here in this nightmare. Playing for keeps.

How was it she hadn't considered death a real possibility until now? She'd heard Harry talk about his escapades. She'd laughed along with him. He'd had fun on many of them.

Not once had he let on how damn dangerous or scary they were.

Well, she knew now.

Mason wrapped his arm around her and pulled her close. He kept up the conversation with Hawk.

"Do we have info on this town?"

"Yes, it's on the maps. Settled about sixty years ago."

Mason nodded. "Residents?"

"A couple of hundred. Mostly men. Older. Some families. A few children."

Right.

Over her head, as if she wasn't even there, they planned sweeps and maneuvers and all she could do was close her eyes and burrow deeper into Mason's chest. God, what was wrong with her?

A man had been killed in front of her. That's what was wrong. Death had become a reality. A distinct possibility now. And quite likely her reality.

Unless these men could save her.

And she had to do what she could to save herself. And them. She didn't think…no…she knew she couldn't get out of here alive on her own. She needed them.

AFTER SYNCING THEIR watches, double checking on their ammunition supplies and once again checking the GPS, all with Tesla burrowed against him, they kept the conversation on point. In truth, Mason was worried about Dane who hadn't checked in on time. He was two minutes late. But if he'd fallen here, there was no way they were leaving him behind. The only alternative was to come back and get him. But Dane was one tough bastard. If there was someone who could get through the entire village in smooth reconnaissance it was him. Dane was silent, experienced and lethal.

He needed time to do his thing.

And they were going to give it to him.

At the hand signal from Hawk, saying Dane had checked in and all was good, Mason glanced down at Tesla. Her arms were wrapped around her knees and, she was huddled in on herself.

Hawk motioned to her feet and the bloody remnants of the

socks. Mason's lips thinned. Damned. The side of her head had been bleeding freely, leaving drying runs of blood on her cheeks. They'd be easy to track with the blood trail they were leaving behind. Still, she didn't complain. That girl had guts.

"Did I see her step in front of you?" Hawk asked Mason in low tones, barely even a whisper.

Tesla never shifted and didn't give any sign she'd heard anything.

Mason wrapped his arms around her, his hand gently covered her one exposed ear. He nodded to Hawk. "And tried to talk the asshole out of killing me."

Hawk shook his head. "Damn. That's some woman. Why would she do that?"

"We can keep her safe? We are her only chance? She identifies with us as her pack?" He whispered the ideas that came to mind.

"She wasn't trying to save all of us. She was saving you."

"Only because I was the one there at the time," he said in a dismissive manner. The last thing he wanted was for the others to think there was anything special between them. Except they already did, given their earlier comments.

"She's worth it."

He nodded. "Since when did you care?" With a casual deflection, he asked Hawk about the tall leggy dark haired beauty he'd spent his last leave with. "What happened to your last lovely?"

Hawk grinned. "Everything I could manage in the time given. As I have with every other one. Still, over time they all do tend to blend into a continuous roll of beauties."

"Life's tough," Mason mocked but he understood. Life as a

SEAL offered a continuous buffet of willing beauties. But over time…they stopped being special.

"Ha, you should know. You were doing plenty of enjoying yourself over the last few years."

Mason smiled. True enough.

"Until what, about a year ago?" Hawk was puzzling his way through the concept of Mason being a changed man and just what would do something like that to him. Mason hoped he didn't get that far.

"Until Harry's death." Hawk grinned as he figured it out.

Mason's gaze snapped to Tesla. But he needn't have worried. She was still in the same position and appeared to be sleeping. He worried about her. Had done so for months. Since Harry's death. He'd always been fascinated with the tales Harry had shared. He'd had no idea if Harry would have approved of him taking an interest. He'd been pretty careful to keep his attraction to himself. That had been easy as there'd always been women available. They had been an enjoyable way to pass the time, and a way to keep his dreams to himself. Until he'd lost Harry.

And with Harry's death came that second look at life and what was important and what did he want to do before the land mine with his name on it found him. At the same time he'd had that insidious idea that with Harry out of the picture there was no barrier to meeting her and seeing where it went. Now though, he realized that Harry was between them more than ever.

"Right?"

He glanced back at Hawk and caught his wide grin as he mentally went click, click, click and came up with the right answer.

Hawk made a silent *oh* sound with his mouth and his gaze

widened in sudden awareness, his gaze intent on Tesla and the way she was snuggled into his chest.

But he stayed quiet. For which Mason was grateful.

He checked the time. "Go time."

Hawk stepped up and front, Mason shook Tesla awake. "Tesla. Time to go. You can rest in a few moments. Let's get you to safety. Then you can rest."

She opened her eyes, dark bruises underneath. His heart melted a little. She'd been such a trooper. "Come on."

"Okay," she said in a soft voice. "I'm ready."

But she wasn't standing on her own two feet yet. In fact, he wasn't sure she could stand without his assistance. He patted her cheeks gently. "We need to go now."

She blinked, then gave a head shake. "Okay, let's go." She turned and stumbled out of his arms and behind Hawk. That she never said a word said much about her mental state.

There's no way she'd be able to walk on those bloody stumps without crying out. They were either numb – not good – or she was – also not good.

Besides, she was leaving a visible blood trail.

Hawk caught his attention and motioned to Tesla. Mason nodded. He scooped her up and fell into line.

This had to end soon. Or she wasn't going to make it.

CHAPTER 7

T HE REST OF that trip was a blur. She knew they'd walked miles. There'd been a meeting up with another member of the team before she was carried to a small dilapidated house just outside the edge of town. She had no idea who lived there, if anyone, and couldn't work up the energy to care.

There was a bathroom. A real one with a toilet and a bathtub. The men had also somehow, from somewhere, rummaged up food. She had a real meal. She felt almost normal now. Supposedly she was going to be picked up by a group tomorrow morning. Soon this nightmare would be over. She could sleep for days if she wanted to then. Mission accomplished.

That worked for her.

Now if only she could get to that bath, then bed part of this mess.

"Eat." Mason stared down at her half empty plate. "You need your strength."

Strength. Right. Eat even if you don't want to. It's food. It's energy. Her father's words rattled through her skull. She picked up her fork again and forced another bite down. She did need food. And a bath.

She brightened. If she finished eating, she could squeeze a bath in before she collapsed. Then again, she had to make it to the bath first. Just then, Mason nudged her elbow. She lifted her tired gaze to him.

"Come on. Bedtime."

She shook her head. "Bath first."

He nodded. "Let's go." He stood up and picked her up.

"Whoa," she cried. "I can walk."

He snorted. "If that was the case then you'd have made your way up there before now."

She groaned. "I was working up the energy for the trip."

He carried her up the stairs and into the small quaint bathroom. Putting her on the counter, he swiveled and quickly turned on the water to fill a bath for her. She smiled. Had anything ever looked so good?

They both stared as the tub filled halfway. He reached down and switched off the water. Rummaging around in the cupboard, he quickly found her an old towel. Then turned to face her.

She snickered. "Yes, I'm fine. Yes, I can get in on my own. Yes, I will call you if I run into trouble."

His laughter rang through the bathroom.

"See, I'm learning." She grinned impishly. Nothing could knock her mood right now. She was inside, safe with a bathtub full of hot water waiting for her. Life was good.

Besides, there was the sexiest man she'd ever met standing beside her. And he appeared to care about her wellbeing. Might be just because of the job...but...

He dropped a kiss on her forehead and walked out, leaving her alone, her fingers reaching up to touch the spot he'd kissed. Why had he done that? Again? Surely he hadn't meant it. Or rather he saw her as Harry's little sister and therefore was going to treat her the same way.

She slid off the counter, wincing as her damaged feet hit the cold linoleum floor. Getting into the water was going to hurt, yet they were in desperate need of a hot soak and cleaning. As was the rest of her. She stripped off her ruined clothes, wondering if there was anything left behind in the house she could wear. She couldn't imagine putting on her destroyed bloodstained clothing again. There were more holes than material left.

Perched on the side of the bath, she gently slipped her feet in the warm water. Tears came to her eyes at the stinging. It felt good but that sting quickly became a scorching burn. She closed her eyes and tried to breathe through it. After a couple of long moments, she slid the rest of the way into the water, this time gasping in joy as her aching muscles were enveloped in the comforting heat.

She had no idea how much time she had but took several minutes to lie submerged, letting the heat wash over her hair and face. Then she went about the painful business of wetting down her hair and trying to clean it with the bar of soap. She was dusty and bloody and damn it, every inch hurt.

By the time she was done, she was exhausted. She managed to hitch herself up to the side of the bathtub again to snag up the towel on the floor. The dry rough textured material made short work of the moisture still clinging to her skin. She redressed in her underclothes and wrapped the towel around her while contemplating her options. She could walk out to the bedroom in a towel and hope to make it into her room sight unseen. Or she could call out for help and get carried into her room, thus letting her feet stay clean. If there was more medicated ointment, her feet could really use it and needed to be clean before putting it on. If not, then it didn't matter. Then again, clean feet would heal better and that was her prime requirement right now. Healing.

She called out, "Mason?"

There was a quick tap on the door then it opened and he popped his head around. Saw her sitting wrapped up in a towel and nodded. "Good idea."

He walked in, picked her up, towel and all and said, "I've got the ointment sitting beside the bed. We'll get that on first then you can go to sleep."

"Any chance of a change of clothes?" she asked hopefully. "There's not much left of mine."

"I'll be able to find you a t-shirt. Not sure if any of our pants would fit. Definitely no underclothes."

"I'm wearing those, but my t-shirt, sweater, and jeans are history."

He smiled at her as he laid her down. "I'll take a look after we get your feet taken care of."

Taking care of her feet took longer and required more effort than she'd thought. Now clean, the tissue was raw and swollen. He dressed both, then leaving her lying on the bed, he left to search for more clothes.

She dropped the towel to the floor and managed to shift under the blankets. He could look for clothes all he liked. She was looking for sleep.

Closing her eyes, she slowly relaxed. Thank God this was over.

NO MORE THAN ten minutes later, Mason came back to find her sleeping heavily in the bed. With the towel on the floor, her body tucked under the sheets, he had to grin at her feet sticking straight out so the ointment wouldn't muck up the bedding. He had no such qualms himself, but it was such a feminine thing to do it made him smile.

A quick trek to the bathroom had him bringing the rest of her clothes, and making sure there was nothing else left behind, he quickly packed up her useless clothing into the bottom of his pack. They wanted nothing to remain of their passing through here. And definitely nothing to say Tesla had been here.

They were running two hour rotating watches. He was on outside watch next. Swede stepped through the bedroom doorway to stand guard over Tesla, saw her bloody feet sticking out of the covers while the rest of her was buried under the blankets and said, "Small feet."

Mason agreed. "Back in four hours."

"I'll be here. Go, she'll be fine."

With a last glance at sleeping beauty, Mason headed out to relieve Hawk.

Sitting up in the tree from the far corner of the property they had a perfect coverage of the house and particularly the corner where Tesla slept.

"Go. I'm here."

Hawk nodded and skimmed down the tree. He was half squirrel the way he could move his body along the trees. He also climbed better than any of them.

"It's all clear." He sprinted to the front of the house where Shadow was on guard. All angles had to be covered. He'd switched places with Hawk in two hours so they were always moving someone around.

Mason leaned back and let his nose take in the scent of the

night. The only way to survive sessions like this was to be one with it. That meant letting go of everything in his mind, in his head. Let it all drift away, drop the worries but sharpen the senses. With his next breath out, he released his attachment to the moment and let the experience of the tree, the night, the air sink inside. It helped him to hear movement on the ground, noises in the wind. It allowed for so much more sensory knowledge that he never did a guard watch without it.

He swiveled his head to the left. Something moved. With his eyes closed he worked to identify it. A deer. He smiled at the size of the buck. That guy had better keep on moving or he'd end up on a hunter's dinner table before too long. It might not be hunting season, but many people living in the back country helped themselves to Mother Nature's bounty. Regardless of the law.

Relaxing deeper, he could hear the sounds of running water up ahead. There must be a creek. Good, they could use that to their advantage if they needed to.

He set his GPS locator and settled back for his watch.

It went quickly. The night was silent. At peace. With any luck Tesla slept, and they could get her moved out to safety. She deserved it. And him, well he'd head back to base and await new orders.

Like he always did.

He saw Hawk switch with Swede at Tesla's doorway. Good. Watch time. Swede moved out to the base of the tree. Swede was big and not a tree climber by choice, but he'd find a place that worked for him and use that for his watch. They all had their own system.

Mason shimmied down and nodded to Swede. He slipped to

the front of the house and cocked an ear. All clear.

He entered the house and walked up to Tesla's bedroom. Hawk waited for him.

"She's been sleeping solid."

"Good, it's what she needs."

Hawk nodded and slipped away. Mason would catch a few hours of sleep, then go relieve someone out front. The system worked better than most and worked because they all knew what they were doing and why.

He'd never had a problem with anyone on his team. Their lives depended on each other. And apparently on those they were rescuing if Tesla's actions today were anything to go by.

He smiled at her position. Had she moved at all? She was still flung across the bed, her feet still sticking out and her head buried under the covers.

Good. A sleep like that was exactly what she needed.

Now he needed to catch some rest himself.

Then tomorrow, he'd be able to meet up and hand her over.

That was what this was all about.

Collect the package before anyone else could.

He'd done that and more.

It was almost time to let go.

And that he realized with shock was something he didn't want to do. A first for him. A first for any woman in his life. He'd had plenty of short term relationships. They all had. A group of women hung around the bars in the hopes of catching themselves a SEAL. Often he and the team let themselves be caught. After all, why not? Life was for living, and hey, women made the living a whole lot sweeter. But it was also getting old.

He glanced back over at the sleeping woman.

Still, it's not like his interest would come to anything.

How could it? His lifestyle was dangerous as all hell, and she'd already lost someone to the war. She wasn't going to be interested in facing the danger of a second one.

Military lifestyle was hell on partners.

CHAPTER 8

S HE WOKE TO heat, a hot stifling type of heat. She sat up, threw off the covers and breathed deep as the cool air of the night flowed over her hot skin.

"Easy, Tesla, take it easy."

"Hot. So hot," she muttered, flopping back on the mattress. She kicked the bedding off her legs, trying to cool down yet again. A warm hand touched her forehead.

She twisted away from him. "I'm hot, don't add your hot hand to my head," she cried. "Why is it so hot?"

In the background she could hear someone whisper, "Shit."

She didn't know what his problem was. She was the one who was hot. Then she realized she wasn't alone. "Are you hot too?" She turned feverish eyes to Mason and studied him. He looked normal. But then normal for him was hot. "No. You're already hot. It can't be bothering you."

He frowned. "What?"

"Why are you so hot?" she cried. "I'm hot too but not hot like you are."

He shook his head.

She frowned up at him. "Of course you're hot," she snapped as she rolled over onto her stomach and stretched out across the whole mattress. "That's better."

"What's better?" Mason asked beside her.

"This waterbed. It's much cooler."

Then he touched her feet. She screeched in pain, flipped over onto her back and burst into tears. "Why are they burning? They are on fire. Why? Can't you put the fire out," she pleaded with him.

"I will. You stay here and I'll get water."

"Water. Yes. Water. It would put out the flames," she cried. "Hurry."

She twisted in pain, her knees bending and straightening as the throbbing wouldn't stop.

She whimpered, but it caught in the back of her throat and ended up sounding like a gurgle. She half laughed. "That sounded bad. I'm not sick. I'm just so hot."

"You're running a fever," said a grim voice beside her.

She opened her eyes and shrieked. Mason was leaning over her, his face close to hers, his gaze locked on her, cataloguing her features.

"Water," she asked when she could. "I'm so thirsty."

"Here." He reached an arm under her shoulders and helped her to sit up. Holding the glass to her lips, she drank greedily. When the glass was empty, she sank back to the pillows, tugging the covers up to hide the bare skin her underwear didn't cover. Then immediately, threw the covers off again. It was too hot.

"Sorry," she whispered.

"Really," he said, a smile in his voice. "What are you sorry about?"

"I got sick. You don't need that."

"Well, at least you got sick at the right time. You'll be taken out of here and get medical help within a few hours. Now if you'd been so inclined as to have gotten sick earlier, well that's a different story. But we're safe right now."

She gave him the briefest of smiles, appreciating his sense of humor.

"However, I have to clean your feet again," he said. "So I'm going to retrieve the stuff I need then I'll be back."

"And I won't be here," she muttered. "I don't want anyone to touch them."

"They are the reason for the fever, so it doesn't matter what you want," he said, his voice hard. Determined.

Instantly tears jumped into her eyes. She turned her face into the pillows to hide them.

Still hot and hating the weakness washing over her, she rolled all the way over until she was lying on her side, curled up in fetal position. He'd do it regardless of her feelings or the pain. The sane part of her mind said it needed to be done. She was sick and that was holding them all back. If she could feel better, she'd be able to run again, even if it was just to the right vehicle. Having her mobility stripped away from her made her feel vulnerable. Victimized. Weak. She needed her feet to heal.

That meant letting him treat them.

When she heard footsteps returning, she buried her face in the pillow and clenched the cotton casing tight in her fists.

There was no way she wanted to talk to him.

Her foot was grabbed in a firm hand and lifted. Nerves had her instinctively pulling it back.

Instantly, other hands grabbed her bare calf and stretched it out. Holding it firm.

She froze.

"Tesla. Swede is going to hold your legs down so I can do

this. Bite on the pillow. It will help you deal with the pain."

She snorted.

"Swede."

Instantly her body was shifted like she was a two-year-old until her legs were supported by the bed and only her feet were hanging over the end. She lay on top of a rough scratchy surface, the top blanket, it was so rough she instantly shifted to rest her head on her folded arms. A blanket was thrown over her.

Damn it. It was hot, too.

The bed sagged as Swede, at least she presumed it was him, sat down. She could hear the two of them mutter, but her own nerves, that horrible anticipation of oncoming pain blocked out any semblance of understanding. She started to shake.

"Okay, I'm going to start."

Swede reached down and gripped both ankles firm against the edge the bed.

Cool water poured over her feet.

Her relief was palpable as the light liquid didn't hurt – until the burn set in. She clenched her jaw and arched her back as the shock and agony ripped through.

But she never made a sound.

Somewhere in the back of her brain, all she could remember was his earlier message about needing to be quiet. But she wanted to cry. She wanted to scream. Truly, she wanted to bawl her pain away. But held back. Locked into her position, her back arched, her arms rigid as her body fought against the agony.

"Jesus," Swede said. "Hurry up."

"I'm trying," Mason muttered.

Whatever he did next brought her collapsing back down on the bed. She closed her eyes…and endured.

MASON LOOKED UP at Swede then motioned toward Tesla's head. "Is she out?" he said in a low voice. He figured she had to be as her feet lay soft and pliant in his hands. Since that first reaction she hadn't moved.

Swede shook his head. "Her eyes are open."

Shocked, Mason stretched up to take a look. Sure enough, she stared across the room to the wall on the other side. And a small steady stream of tears rolled down her cheeks.

But she never made a sound.

Affected more than he'd have thought possible, he gritted his jaw closed and returned to the task at hand. This was hurting him as much as her. And from the grim look on Swede's face, he knew the big mammoth wasn't unaffected either.

He took his time to make sure all the slivers and grime were out of the torn flesh. This time he dug deep, spreading the sliced flesh and cleaned. He hadn't seen them all before and had missed several cuts. Now there was no room for error. She had everything from tiny pebbles buried in the puffy flesh to slivers. He thought there were tiny slivers of glass but couldn't imagine from where. By the time he was done, blood ran freely down her foot. Knowing it was going to hurt, but not having much option, he dumped the last of the alcohol over her bare feet.

They jerked and twitched. Glancing upward he could see her white fingers grimly clenching the damn blankets, but she never made a sound. Her eyes though, Lord the look of pain almost broke his heart.

Swede handed him the bandages, cut up sheets had been sacrificed for the job.

Accepting them, he acknowledged the other man's need to leave too. They both wanted to be done here. Torturing kittens was something they'd beat up another man for. But when they had to do it themselves... Well, neither man wanted any part of it.

Determined to make sure her feet would heal now, he smeared ointment across them then bandaged first one then the other. He carefully bound her feet and ankles, needing the bandages to be snug but not so tight as to hurt.

She might want to run away, but she'd be lucky to hobble anywhere for several days.

Would she hold her condition against him? She should.

He did.

CHAPTER 9

S HE WASN'T SURE at what point in the process she'd dropped into the dead zone. The point where she was still conscious but no longer concerned herself with the outside world as she was so focused on staying strong inside.

Her father had talked to her about it. Warned her that under horrible conditions, he'd often had to go there just to keep alive. Although she'd come close to that point in the cabin, tied up and lost, she'd still been outside. This time, with silence being paramount, she'd gone inside easily.

He'd been right. It was the place to go to survive.

She'd never have made it through that torture otherwise.

Even calling it torture made her wince. It was hardly that. But it had been painful as hell. Nothing compared to the psychos out there who really were into torture, but it had been enough for her. She couldn't imagine if she was captured and taken overseas. She didn't think she'd survive. She wasn't like the strong men who'd rescued her. She couldn't imagine the training they must have gone through.

She hoped she'd never have to go through anything worse than this. She almost laughed but as she was still not moving her feet in case they started pounding with pain, any sudden movement was out of the question.

She wiped her eyes on the sheet beneath her cheek, thankful the tears were long gone. She knew they'd have noticed. How could they not? But there were only so many things she could worry about.

Tears didn't make it on that list.

But bawling like a weak wuss did.

She couldn't remember how she'd been during the process. Hopefully she hadn't shamed Harry or her father too much.

If she had, too damn bad. She was Tesla. Not their clones. She'd do her best, and if she didn't match up to their expectations then...well, it wasn't the first time.

A gentle hand lowered onto her shoulder.

"How are you feeling?"

The voice so close to her ear made her freeze. Slowly she raised her head and looked around. Not only was she no longer crosswise on her bed, she was lying normally on one side, her feet propped up on pillows, the rest of her body covered by blankets. Her gaze slowly moved from her propped up feet to Mason's jean covered legs and...she swallowed as her gaze wandered higher to his bare heavily muscled torso, up to the broad shoulders and his shadowed features, the narrow gaze full of concern...for her.

She wanted to smile.

Sexiest looking man ever. In her bed. And not for her. But *because* of her. Sigh. She managed a wan smile. "From the look on your face I guess I was in rough shape?"

His features relaxed and he lay back down on the bed. "You could say that. But looks like you're back."

He propped his arms under his head, but his gaze never wavered as he studied her face. Her face that felt like it had been pummeled with a hammer, hot, swollen.

"I am." Now if only she understood where she'd been. She remembered a lot of last night. But not all of it. Evidently she'd dropped off to sleep at some point. She felt better. But a long way away from good yet. She forced her gaze away from his massive arms and stared down at the pillow in front of her. Tear stained, it showed the evidence of a hard night.

"Sorry for worrying you."

He sat up, dropping his hands to rest on his knees. "Oh, we were worried all right. The fever broke finally, and I think we got that mess out of your feet."

"Is that what the problem was?" Her gaze cut over to his. "My feet?"

"Yeah. Not sure if it was the slivers that were in there, the rocks you had embedded, or you'd been bitten. Honestly, they were so swollen, I couldn't tell."

Her eyebrows shot up. "Really?" At his nod, she twisted around to take a more careful look at the bandages.

"So no dancing today, huh?"

His grin was wide and devilish. "Not unless it's lap dancing."

"Oh." She blushed hot. "I'll forego that pleasure for a while, thanks."

"Too bad." He hopped to his feet, bare feet, she registered at the last moment. "However, there are other priorities to consider."

She struggled to sit up, relieved to see her bra and panties on. They covered more of her then her bikini. She was willing to overlook the feeling that they were more intimate. She flipped so she was sitting on her butt and checked out the room. It was the same as the one she'd gone to bed in. Good. At least she recognized her surroundings and that meant the bathroom was around the corner.

Damn.

As if understanding the uncertain woebegone look on her face, he walked around to her side of the bed and held out his arms. "Grab a hold."

Flushing with embarrassment, she reached her arms around his neck and let him carry her to the bathroom. There he slowly lowered her to the toilet seat then stood there uncertainly.

"I'm fine," she said hurriedly.

He narrowed his gaze and nodded. "I'll let you try but if you can't manage on your own…"

Her face now scarlet, and shaking wildly in denial of what he hadn't said, she waited until he walked to the doorway and pulled the door partly closed. Without too much effort, she managed to shuffle her cotton panties down over her cheeks so she could relieve herself. She even managed to finish the job and get the panties back up. But the sink looked too damn far away to wash her hands. She was going to have to stand up.

Taking a deep breath, she slowly lowered her feet to the floor and using the toilet for support she pushed herself upright. And gasped. Choking back the other sounds threatening to rush out of her mouth, she swayed in place for a long moment while she adjusted to the pain and weird feeling of walking on flesh that felt twice the size it should be. But she could stand. And given the options, she'd take it. And if she could stand, she could walk.

She took one careful step and then another. With her legs braced against the cupboard and her elbows braced on the counter, she could wash her hands. Splashing water on her face, she felt much better. Turning, she looked into Mason's face now standing in the open doorway frowning at her.

"I know," she said gently. "You'd have helped me. But I needed to see how bad they were."

The frown eased slightly. "I can understand that. But now back to bed."

She nodded and this time, knowing what she could do and couldn't, she reached out her arms. He was there in a single stride and swung her up against his chest. Back in the bedroom, he laid her down again.

"When am I being picked up?" she asked, pulling the blankets over her chest. A chill was settling in after just that little bit of movement. It didn't say much for the day ahead. Not many men would be happy to carry her around. And while he saw her as a job and would do what was required, that didn't mean the next group would. An idea struck. She glanced over at him, "Do you think..." she frowned now rethinking.

"What?"

She winced. "I was just wondering if a wheelchair would be possible once I'm taken out of here."

"As you'll be going to a hospital first to be checked over, then I would think that would be an obvious answer for a day or two. But more likely you'll be confined to bed."

"Damn," she pleated the cotton sheet at her neck.

"What, you don't like lying in bed?"

"Not alone." Her unexpected answer brought a light of interest to his eyes and hot color to her cheeks again.

"That sounds interesting."

She shook her head. "There's nothing interesting about me."

Silence.

"Really?" But the note of incredulity had her frowning up at him.

"Yeah, really."

His gaze searched hers. "Then you need to take another look in the mirror."

She snorted. "I just did, remember."

His grin was huge. "Yeah, you're looking pretty beat up right now."

She rolled her eyes at him, her hand instantly going to the side of her head that stung from the slivers.

"How come I'm the one that is all beat up and you guys are fine," she complained, but in a light tone.

Swede chose that moment to walk into the bedroom.

He carried a huge mug.

She stared at it hopefully. "Is that coffee?"

He nodded.

But he stayed just out of reach.

"Could I have a cup, please?"

He rolled his eyes and stepped to her side and handed her the mug. "Man, you're not even fun to tease right now. It's like beating up a butterfly."

She stopped in the middle of lifting his cup to her lips. A butterfly? She smiled. It could be worse.

MASON MOTIONED SWEDE to the hallway.

"A butterfly?" he asked in low tones. "Really?"

"Yeah." Swede grinned. "She's lovely. And you'll appreciate her more if you have to work for it. Besides, she can't make a choice if she doesn't know she has one."

"Not you, too?" Mason groaned.

"Absolutely. We can recognize special, even if you can't," he said as he walked down the hallway.

"Who says I can't?" Mason snapped.

At his friend's rolling laughter, he realized he'd been had.

Damn. Leaning against the doorjamb he could recognize special just fine. Especially this kind of special. The trick was what was he going to do about it? Nothing. For the same damn reason he'd not gone to see her while Harry was alive or dead. And now that Harry was gone, she deserved to have a husband who was whole and home every day. The SEALs were his life. He'd made that decision a long time ago. It was better for everyone that way.

He turned away and came face to face with Hawk.

"I could have killed you just now. You're so preoccupied with your personal life." He snickered and motioned toward Tesla in bed. "And if you can't see how much of a difference she'd make in your life, you're a fool." And he sauntered inside the room. "Hey, pretty lady. It's my turn to be your guard."

"Do I still need a guard?" Tesla asked. "I thought we were out of danger."

"Until you are safe and sound and back home and these guys caught and dealt with, you aren't out of danger. And let me rephrase. Mason needs a nap."

"Oh dear. I never thought of that. Poor Mason."

Mason rolled his eyes at Hawk's blatant lie and stormed off.

They were all making him crazy.

CHAPTER 10

THEY WERE ALL making her crazy. She was dressed in Shadow's spare pants. Wore Mason's spare shirt and had a rope from Swede's pack to hold up her pants. On her feet she wore two pairs of socks, one from Hawk and one from Dane. They'd all contributed. She laughed at herself in the mirror. She'd never quite fit in with the current fashion but their generosity warmed her heart.

And walking was still horrible. As in seriously painful. But with the bandages and double socks, doable. And that was what counted. Walking slowly on her own steam was way better than being carried. Of course, if Mason gave her his arm to help for balance she wouldn't argue.

He was a cutie.

But he was a SEAL. And had a mess of women at his beck and call. She knew all about it from Harry. Damn good thing she had the insider scoop. And even as a part of her wished she didn't know about them, she knew she'd still *know* about them from the look of them. All the men had that hard, been there and can do it again – blindfolded, look to them. That dangerous power emanating from their very skin as if to say there wasn't anything in the work they couldn't handle – including a woman in their bed. Or many women in their bed. She grinned.

Mason…well, he had something extra special to him.

"Ready?" Mason stood on the other side of the door waiting for her. She'd been sitting on the counter in the bathroom trying to build up the courage to jump down on her feet. It was going to hurt.

"Yes, coming."

"Are you sure? I can carry you?"

She winced. So much for all her courageous talking. She rolled over and slipped down off the counter and landed gently. Taking a deep breath to acclimatize, she walked to the door and lied. "I'm fine."

"Good. The truck is here. And the helicopter is waiting."

At the word helicopter, all the color bleached from her skin. "Helicopter," she said faintly. "Really? Again?"

He nodded. "Look, this time it will be fine."

She stared up at him, willing to be convinced but knowing there was no argument that would be good enough to get the job done. "Are you sure there's no other way?"

He reached out and clasped both elbows. She looked down to see her arms wrapped tightly around her chest, her fingers gripping her arms in a death grip.

"I promise."

She narrowed her gaze. "Really?"

He nodded.

She snorted. "That means you are coming with me, right?"

"Uhm…"

At his hesitation she froze. "That means no, and therefore I'm not going." Good. Decision made. Easy. She'd stay here until another plan could be worked out.

"That's not happening. You have to go. You have to be safe."

"And so do you." She gave a short nod, glanced at the three others standing there, big grins on their faces. "What are you all smirking at?" She raised an eyebrow at them. "Were you the one who threw me out of the last helicopter?"

"No. It was Mason," Swede said, humor coloring his voice.

"Well, I've almost forgiven him for it, but what if this helicopter blows up too? Who's going to clip me to their parachute and save me then?"

As the men glanced at each other, she added, "Exactly."

She turned back to Mason. "And if it's so damn safe, why aren't you coming?"

"It's not big enough for all of us."

"Ha. That's a lie. Helicopters are big."

"This is a little one," he said in exasperation. "And you have to go. They are waiting for you at the base."

"And what if I don't arrive." She shook her head. "No. If one of us goes, then all of us go. No one gets left behind." And she was going to stand firm on that.

The men grinned.

She glared at them. "What is your problem?"

"You," Mason said in irritation. "But we don't have time to argue. And as your feet are too sore, I'll carry you to the vehicle."

She snickered. "Can't keep your hands off me, can you?" She laughed as bright color rolled over his cheeks. But he just sighed and carried her down the stairs. She grinned over his shoulder at Hawk and Swede, the two she could see.

Hawk winked at her.

She laughed. "Your team agrees with me."

"My men are idiots," he muttered. At the front door he stopped and waited for the two men to slip out in front, both going in opposite directions and diving to the sides. Hawk was the last to step out in front of them.

"He could get hurt that way," she said. "If anyone is going to shoot at us, he's going to get hit."

"Exactly. He's trying to keep you from getting hit," Mason said, his voice hard, careful.

She peered into the surrounding area. Swede had already gained entrance to the large SUV and now it was their turn.

Holding her carefully, he ran to the passenger side and placed her in the backseat. While she shifted into a better position, he leaned over and buckled her in.

"Wait, you're coming this far, aren't you?"

He shook his head. "No. Cooper, another of my team, here is driving you to the airfield. Johann is riding shotgun."

Johann? Cooper? She glanced at the driver, not sure she'd seen him before. How many of these SEALs were there?

But she wouldn't let go of him. "No. You have to come to the airfield," she cried. "You can't stay here. It's too dangerous."

"Cooper will come back and pick us up later."

She stared at him, hating to leave. But he seemed to be completely unfazed.

Get a grip, she said to herself. *He doesn't give a shit.* She leaned back and in a cool voice said, "Fine. Thank you for your assistance. Good-bye."

She stared straight ahead, ignoring his start of surprise.

He backed up and slammed the door shut with a little too much force. She sniffled, trying to hold back the tears as Cooper started up the vehicle.

Suddenly her door opened. Mason leaned in. "It's not okay," he snapped. "But it's the job. I'll contact you later."

And he kissed her. As in he placed his lips on hers, her body temperature shot up ten degrees and curled her toes.

Then he backed up and slammed the door in her face.

She gave a happy sigh and settled back for the trip.

He did care.

"HA. DAMN WELL time." Hawk looped an arm around Mason's shoulders. "Told you he wasn't stupid."

Swede smirked. "Of course if he doesn't follow through there's still a chance for us."

The others all agreed.

"She's not up for grabs," Mason snapped. Something was bugging him, but he couldn't place it. Except she was gone and damn if his life didn't seem a little darker. A little cloudier. As if a ray of sunshine had just gone behind a cloud.

Foolish thoughts. He'd get over her like he'd gotten over every other woman he'd met. She was no damn different.

Liar. Christ she was different.

"Let's go. We have things to do and places to be."

"We do indeed." They all stood in place and watched the dark SUV drive away. Dust clouded the air in front of them.

As they watched, another dark SUV pulled out of a hiding spot from deep in the tree-lined road and pulled in behind them.

"No." Mason stared, his heart beating against his chest. "No, please not."

"Oh, Christ," the men whispered in horror.

"Wheels. We need wheels." Swede was already on the phone. "Skip the wheels. I'm bringing in the helicopter."

The men scattered. Except Mason. He watched the two vehicles head down the road.

Then he remembered the old dirt bike he'd seen in the back of the shed. In ten seconds he'd ripped to the shed, flung the door open so hard it came off the hinge and pulled it out. The tank was half full. Good enough. He turned the key sitting in the engine, she fired up. Good baby.

Without giving a second thought, he spun her around and raced off behind Tesla.

Like hell he was going to lose her now.

CHAPTER 11

S HE SLUMPED INTO the buttery leather seat. Tears were clinging to the corner of her eyelids. She sniffled them back. There was no way she was going to let them fall. She didn't dare. The dam would break and she'd bawl like a baby. So not good for her strong-can-handle-anything look. She had one like that... Didn't she? Hell no. She'd *had* one like that way back. Her initial reserve on meeting someone often gave them that impression of her. Cool. Unaffected. Disinterested. And she'd done nothing to break that barrier down to make it easier for everyone. Her father would say show them who's boss right from the get go. Then you could pick and choose who to befriend. That was *after* you figured out who were your enemies.

His method clearly hadn't worked so well in high school and just added to her cool edge.

She stared down at her ragged nails. They'd been perfect pale ovals once. Now they were short, jagged and bloody. She had a couple she could still use as weapons if she had to. But her fighting days were over. Hopefully.

On that reminder, she glanced out the windows. Good-bye small town. Good-bye jaunt in the back woods. Hello more scary helicopter ride and more military.

The military she'd take any day. Now getting back into another helicopter – so not.

Her stomach knotted at the reminder of her free-fall the last time. It would be good to go back in, just like falling off a bike. You had to get back on again immediately.

This was a whole different story. She'd do the bike thing any day. The helicopter, however… She took one deep breath, then another deep breath. The third one almost felt natural.

Until she noticed the driver keeping a careful eye on the road. She knew Mason wouldn't have let her leave if he didn't think it was safe to do so. But what if they were being followed? What if someone had tracked them to the house and was waiting to make their move.

Mason really shouldn't have let her leave alone. She hated that she only felt safe with him beside her. It was understandable after what she'd been through but…that was going to be difficult in the future.

Damn it, her mind was back on Mason again. And that long lovely expanse of bare skin she'd woken up to. She'd always been a morning person. To think he'd been there in her bed, and she didn't have the right to touch. She could have persuaded him…maybe, but she didn't want a ten minute bounce in bed. She wanted to get to know him. Yeah right. She wanted to jump his bones. But she couldn't have handled rejection this morning, and he would have turned her down.

With a groan she leaned her head back, determined to forget the man. And that wicked kiss he'd laid on her.

"You all right, ma'am?" Cooper asked her, concern written on his face.

She mustered up a bright smile. They were all lovely men. "I'm fine. Just not looking forward to going on another helicopter."

"You'll be fine."

Right. She was pretty damn sure she'd been told that right before the last helicopter blew up. But there was no point in bringing that up again.

"I'm sure I will."

The second man pointed at something in his rearview mirror. He had some kind of phone in his hand, but it looked big, odd. More like a GPS unit but with other capabilities. Interesting. She loved technology. She and Harry had both been big on computers growing up.

Now she wished she had something in her hands. She had no phone, or purse, so no ID. She felt cut off from the world.

Especially without Mason.

Then her world exploded.

The first shot shattered the rear window and punctured a hole right through the front windshield.

She screamed and leaned over. That was when she realized Johann's blood was all over the front dash. And Cooper was swearing a blue streak.

Oh no. Oh crap. Oh Lord. *Please not again.* She unbuckled her seatbelt and hit the floor.

"Hang on," Cooper yelled at her.

But the SUV was zigging and zagging so severely across the road as the driver tried to avoid letting the shooter get a clean shot at him that it was damn near impossible to hang on. She leaned forward over the center console where the passenger was slumped and checked if he was breathing. She hadn't seen where he'd been shot, but she didn't need to look twice.

Except...he held a gun in his hand. She reached forward and

pulled it free. It was covered in…yeah, she didn't want to know. She wiped off as much as she could but kept being knocked over with Cooper's evasive maneuvers. She tried to pull herself up enough to look out the back window.

"Stay down," Cooper snapped.

The SUV lurched to the side, taking her with it. Damn it. She crawled to the back of the vehicle, sat up, her head hidden by the rear corner of the big machine. But now she had a clear view out the busted rearview window.

Her gaze narrowed as she realized something else.

She had a clear shot.

Of a man leaning out of the window getting ready to take another shot.

She lifted the pistol. Checking that the safety was off, and using all the techniques she'd applied many times at a target but never in real life, she sighted on her target and pulled the trigger.

The man who'd been leaning out of the front window of the second SUV, weapon in hand, collapsed, his body hanging limp over the passenger door.

"Nice shot," Cooper crowed. "Thank you, ma'am."

"You're welcome," she muttered but had to tear her gaze away from the man she'd killed. She bowed her head and silently apologized then added out loud, "I had to do it. You were trying to kill me."

"And you remember that. We're not out of trouble yet."

She immediately pulled herself together. The SUV had dropped way back now that they were up against firepower. And with any luck there was only a driver in the vehicle too. Only it wasn't to be. As she watched, the passenger door was opened and the dead man tossed out. Another man took his place.

"There's another shooter coming up."

"Damn," Cooper called out. "We've got a bike coming down the hill on the left."

Oh no. She didn't want an innocent bystander getting in the middle of this nightmare. It was probably a teenager doing what he did best – ripping rubber. She could hear the noise of the engine now that Cooper mentioned it. She was peering from the corner of the rearview mirror when a shot fired through the rear window, high but hitting part of the window still hanging, showering her in glass.

"Ack." She flung herself to the floor.

"You okay?" Cooper called, trying to look around for her.

"I'm fine. That was just a little too close."

She slid upwards into the corner again, still hidden but where she could watch as the asshole aimed again. He'd miss her, but he was likely going to hit the tires. Not happening. She couldn't stand to be tossed around any more than she had been.

Besides this was starting to piss her off.

She fired through the shattered window at their windshield. She'd missed. Only the passenger side of the windshield shattered. That just made it easier on them to shoot at her. "God damn it," she muttered. She had to do something. Then she laughed. That part would be easier.

If they were going to shoot out tires, then she would too. That had been one of Harry's favorite targets. Tires on a rope connected to a pulley that he could slow down or speed up. This she could do. She shifted back to get the best aim possible and shot.

Bam. The tire blew and the vehicle swerved, hit a bank, lifted and rolled, coming to a loud stop in the center of the road.

She grinned. Damn right. Take that assholes.

The sound of the bike grew horrifically loud as it jumped a hillock and suddenly landed right behind the SUV. She gasped and shrank back until she saw the military pants and no helmet.

Mason.

She laughed and waved.

The look on his face…yeah someone was going to catch hell.

Cooper was already slowing down and pulling off to the side.

"Uhm, shouldn't we be going to the airport?" she called out to him.

"We will in a few minutes. The guys are here."

Well, she saw Mason, but who knew where the others were. Then she saw an open top Jeep peeling down the road behind them. They had to have been on their tail right from the beginning. Too bad they hadn't figured out she was in trouble before they sent her away. She was going to give them a piece of her mind for putting her through this.

The SUV came to a complete stop. While Cooper checked his buddy over, and she was damn sorry about him, Tesla stayed curled up in the back, the gun tight in her hand. This day hadn't started out as one to die, but it had gone into the toilet since she'd gotten up, so there was no way in hell she was letting go of her only weapon until the world stopped spitting on her.

Mason or no Mason.

And wait until she saw him. She was going to rip a strip off him.

Except…apparently she was going to have to stand in line.

WHEN THE FIRST shooter was taken out by Cooper's partner,

Mason had cheered. He'd been trying his damnedest to get caught up but when the shooting started, being on a bike was a hell of a place to be. Then a second shooter had stepped in and Cooper's partner Johann had blown a tire. Damn good shooting.

Maybe not the way he'd have done things, but he didn't know what weapon Johann had at his disposal either. He still wasn't going to breathe easy until he was sure Tesla was safe. Hopefully she'd had enough sense to stay down and out of the way. Cooper would have been firm but careful with her. He was no fool. Everyone knew how valuable she was to both sides.

No, Tesla would be as safe as they could keep her. But she had to cooperate.

Then she'd seen him. And he'd been so relieved. Until he saw the gun in her hand. What the hell was Cooper doing arming her? That wasn't a fucking toy. Sure, she was Harry's sister and all but…

When he finally parked the bike and raced to the SUV, Cooper hopped out and said, "She's fine."

Mason gave him a clipped nod and said, "I can see that."

But then he stopped. And looked inside the SUV. He stared at the dead man. Then looked at Cooper.

"Johann was taken out on the first shot," Cooper said quietly. "We had no warning."

Still Mason refused to get it. The passenger door opened and Tesla leaned out and grinned.

He glared at her. The Jeep came to a dusty stop beside them.

Tesla laughed and cried and waved at them. "Oh thank heavens – you're all safe."

Cooper said, "She's the one who took down Johann's shooter."

Mason shook his head.

Cooper nodded. "And she popped their tire. Honest to God, she saved my life."

"Ha." Tesla laughed. "You saved mine so we're even."

Hawk came to the open door and held out his arms. Mason snorted as Tesla fell into them. She appeared to like being carried around – at times at least.

"Thank you for being so smart, so talented, and so damn capable," Hawk said and hugged her hard against his chest.

Then he tossed her to Swede.

CHAPTER 12

WITH A SHRIEK she found herself midair then suddenly caught up in Swede's huge arms. She wrapped her arms around his neck and hugged him back. She was so damned glad they were all here with her. He passed her over to Shadow and the process repeated itself until Mason was the only man left who hadn't hugged her. Dane held her out to Mason, only she refused to be tossed. Instead, she reached out and smacked Mason across the face.

Instant silence.

Then she got in his face and snapped, "And that was for sending me off to get shot when you knew I wasn't going to be safe."

"How the hell was I to know you weren't going to be safe?" he roared, rubbing his cheek, glaring at her.

"Because you weren't there to look after me," she yelled, her nose inches from his.

She snorted and settled back into Dane's arms. And turned away. Only to realize every last one of them were either laughing or grinning at her.

With a narrow gaze she glared at them. Then turned back to Mason. He was staring at her like he had no idea what to do. She gave him a fat smile. "Time to apologize, Mason."

"Apologize?" He got a thunderous look on his face. "For what?"

"For putting me in danger – again," she emphasized.

Swede lost it behind her and backed away guffawing like an idiot. Hawk was bent over and no one dared look at Mason. Well, she had no such qualms. "You don't scare me," she scoffed. "You're a big teddy bear."

That did it, the rest of the men who'd barely held in their laugher cracked up.

Mason snatched her out of Dane's arms. And kissed her. Hard. Hot and long.

She responded enthusiastically. When he finally came up for air, she sagged against him. He said, "At least I've finally found a way to shut you up."

Not knowing where the attitude came from, she smirked and said, "Never."

He rolled his eyes, shifted her in his arms, and said, "I'm sorry for putting you in danger. I thought you'd be safe."

She sniffed.

He glared.

She grinned. "Apology accepted."

He kissed her again.

The others cheered.

DAMN WOMAN. SHE had one job. To stay safe. And what did she do – get herself into a gunfight. Then picked up the gun and actively went after the shooter.

And what to do with her now? Cooper was all about getting her to the airstrip. Hawk had tried to contact the helicopter but wasn't raising a response. Dane was currently trying to contact their base.

He gently replaced Tesla on the seat and turned to face Swede. He'd gone back to the flipped vehicle. At his questioning look, Swede shook his head. Well, that was one way to deal with the enemy, wipe them out. Only he knew that they didn't wipe out easy. Every morning he woke up to find they'd multiplied overnight.

Still, he didn't need to let Tesla know she'd killed three men. The accident would be found soon, and they needed to be away. Swede and Shadow had cleaned the house. The Jeep was packed. He didn't ask where it had come from. They all did what they had to do. Hopefully not damaging this one and getting it back to its rightful owners was an option this time.

His team would bring the Jeep. Mason was going to drive the SUV with Tesla and Cooper would ride shotgun. Dane was coming with them. Three men in each.

Cooper held out his communicator to Mason. Still no answer at the helicopter.

Damn. The landing site had to have been compromised. Still, they had to go check. Swede had a helicopter's pilot license and could fly them out, if it was still there. What they had to do was expect unfriendlies.

At his word, they headed out. The drive was done in complete silence. Mason kept his eye out for any other traffic while Cooper watched for the enemy. Johann's body was in the back, covered with a sheet.

It was Tesla who worried Mason. She hadn't said a word.

After watching the men carry Johann to the back, she'd fallen silent and turned to look out the window. Now she watched the miles drift by but never moved or spoke. Killing wasn't easy for any of them, but they'd adapted out of necessity. For Tesla, this was a first for her – and therefore the hardest. She should never have been put into this position. Taking a life was something she'd never forget. And could spend a lifetime adjusting to. Even though her actions had been fully justified…it would hurt for a long time.

The landing site was at an older bushwhacker style landing strip. The trip there was uneventful with the turnoff to their destination nothing but a small dirt road that appeared deserted. But they knew better at this point.

Guns ready, they drove close to the small shack standing at one end and parked. The Jeep hung well back with Swede, Hawk and Dane. Mason explained that they were going to park in the trees and approach the helicopter by foot.

Mason stepped out of the SUV, glanced over at Tesla to see her huge eyes staring at him. Trusting him.

Damn she was something.

"I'll go look inside." Cooper headed to the doorway and stepped in. He walked out a moment later. "It's empty."

Mason nodded. He'd expected nothing less.

The helicopter sat quiet unattended to the left.

The pilot missing.

Mason took in the long grass around the airstrip. Lots of places to hide.

Cooper rummaged through the hanger then walked back. "Doesn't look like there's anything of value there."

"Right."

"Do we just go up to the helicopter?" Tesla asked from inside the SUV.

"No," Mason said quietly, his gaze moving steadily around them. His senses were saying something had happened, but there wasn't a sense of immediate danger. As if whatever had happened at this place was over and done with. Had the pilot been taken?

A birdcall from behind the helicopter had him searching the area. Finally, Hawk gave the all clear sign and the death call. As it wasn't one of the team, it was for the pilot. "Come on. We're heading to the helicopter now."

"Is the pilot there?"

Mason shook his head. Well, he was likely dead in the back of the helicopter. Hawk would have moved him back out of sight if he could.

Gun at the ready, he approached the machine, Tesla behind him on Cooper's arm and Dane keeping her safe between them. Shadow popped up at the pilot's seat. "She's completely empty."

"Where's the pilot?" Swede growled. "This thing didn't fly in on itself."

"Is it even yours?" asked Tesla in a tart voice. "Did you consider that it might belong to someone else? You can't just take anything anytime, you know."

Mason rolled his eyes. Dane just grinned. Cooper tried to explain. "This is a government helicopter. It's one of ours and this is a tiny airfield meant for small planes not helicopters."

As he finished, Mason glanced over at Tesla. She didn't look like she believed him but was allowing Cooper to help her up into a seat. He could see the pale color of her skin. She was determined to do the right thing. Even if that meant climbing back into the helicopter.

Only her fingers were locked together so tight her knuckles were white. She was terrified. Out of consideration, he snagged one of the parachutes packed into the locker and dropped it beside her.

She stared at it like it was going to bite her.

"Would you rather have one in case or have the case to need it but not have one."

She snatched it up and held it tight to her chest but shot him a menacing glance. "I'd better not need one."

Swede turned to glance at her from the pilot seat. "I've never lost a machine yet."

At that she smiled. "Thanks, Swede."

"What, he gets a thanks and I give you something that could save your life and I get threats," Mason mocked, happy to see her relaxing. Swede had told the truth but that didn't mean he hadn't flown a heavily bullet riddled machine back a time or two. But Mason would keep that information to himself.

CHAPTER 13

TESLA COULDN'T BELIEVE where she was. She was really back in a helicopter and again with unfriendlies around them. They'd taken off ten minutes ago. With Swede flying the machine. Why the original pilot had been killed she had no idea. It must mean the unfriendlies thought they'd be grounded or maybe they had their own pilot. Or hell, maybe they had another way to get what they wanted away from here. She didn't know. She couldn't help but wonder if she'd killed the pilot who'd planned to fly this machine with her as his captive.

It was hard to feel sorry for what she'd done. They'd been trying to kill her – or at least Cooper. And they'd killed Johann. She'd done what she'd had to. But she wished she hadn't been in a position where that had been the best answer. All she wanted was to get home.

In the background she heard the men talking.

"We have contact with the commander. He wants us to fly straight to the base. Deal with the rest from there."

Made sense to her. She'd like nothing better than to be on base right now.

She'd be safe there.

But what would happen to Mason if she were there. Sent off on another mission? To rescue some other damsel in distress. Did he connect with all of them? Or just her? She hoped with none of them.

Hawk sat down beside her. She glanced over, saw his grin and smiled back. Nice guys. All of them.

"We've got about forty minutes then we should be there."

She nodded and shifted the parachute in her lap. Forty minutes was a long time. She'd hang onto it just in case. At this point she just wanted this over.

Her feet were killing her. She needed to get them up to ease the booming throb, but there was no place. She couldn't stop moving them restlessly though, and she was starting to feel lightheaded. When had she eaten last? Forty minutes was starting to sound like a really long time. She glanced behind her where Mason was talking to Cooper. They were sitting on the floor. If she lay down, she could rest her feet on the pack she was clutching. But that would mean getting up, so she'd sit. She shifted her feet again.

Hawk got up and went to the back. Seconds later Mason took his place. He reached down and grabbed her feet and pivoted her so she was sideways in the seat, but her feet were slightly elevated onto his lap. She had to wiggle into a better position to support herself, but the easing of the pain was such a relief she was happy to ignore his highhanded actions. Modern day warriors were still throwbacks to another age.

When she sagged against the side of the helicopter, he asked, "Better?"

She nodded. "Yes, thank you."

He held her feet until Swede called him to the front. She opened her eyes, wondering if she'd been sleeping but figured she'd likely just been in that lovely half awake state.

She could see buildings below. They were arriving. Excitement brightened her spirits.

The helicopter set down carefully. Within minutes they were overrun with people. Why? Medics first and she was checked over then picked up and transported onto a stretcher. "I don't need a stretcher," she snapped, horrified at the spectacle they were making of her. "I'm not an invalid. And neither am I that badly hurt. You need the stretchers for the two fallen men."

At her words the two men who were moving her to an ambulance looked at each other, then down at her. "We'll deal with them in a moment. We take care of the living first."

She was still spluttering when they popped a strap across her hips and chest. And she lost it.

Then she started screaming. "Mason!"

The men bundled her into the ambulance as she fought the straps and them. Now she was fighting in earnest and screaming. "Let me go. Get this off me."

In her mind she didn't know if the men were there to help her or hurt her, but they hadn't been vetted by Mason so who the hell knew?

Suddenly Mason was there. He stood over her. "Easy, Tesla. Take it easy."

She clutched at him, her fingers digging into his arm. "Who are these men? What do they want with me?"

Swede arrived at her other side. Hawk and the others surrounded the stretcher. Hawk immediately unclipped her buckles while Mason lit into the poor men about their callous behavior.

After he finished, the two men threw up their hands and walked away. "We're just following orders."

"Then next time maybe do them with an ounce of compassion," Mason snarled. "She's just come in from being kidnapped, tied up and damn near blown up."

"Hence, the damn stretcher. We were told she couldn't walk."

Tesla gasped and sat up. "You didn't even ask me. My feet are painful to walk on but I'm ambulatory."

"Ha," Mason said. "You could lie here and make this easy on everyone."

She glared at him.

"Uh oh." Hawk smirked. "Now you've done it."

She opened her mouth, and Mason placed a finger against her lips. "Remember, I know how to close this."

Heat flamed over her cheeks, getting hotter as she heard Hawk's strangled chuckles. Her mouth snapped shut and she lay back down. But her gaze, yeah, it promised retribution. But not when there were a dozen strangers watching.

"Good choice." Mason motioned to the men. "Take her in. But no straps," he warned.

When he stepped back. She reached out for his hand. She tugged him lower. He bent over. "Are these men okay?" she whispered.

THE FEAR IN her voice made his heart break. She'd been trying so hard to be brave, but the straps had done her in. "Yes," he said, his voice low, gentle. "You can trust them."

She dropped his hand and relaxed. "I knew that."

He grinned. And couldn't help himself. As the men went to wheel her away, he dropped a hard kiss on her lips, whispering, "You got this."

Her smile was breathtaking.

And he was such a sap.

He brushed past his men, all of them smirking at him.

"Let us know."

"Let you know what?" he turned to face them.

"If you're keeping her," Swede said, a serious tone to his voice belied by the grin on his face.

"Why?" he said, narrowing his gaze at the men he'd known had bedded hundreds of women between them.

"'Cause, if not," Hawk said, sauntering past, "I am."

"Not if I get her first," chimed in Shadow.

Mason snapped. "None of you are keeping her."

Swede, his voice calm yet serious said, "If you're fool enough to let her go, you can bet we aren't."

"Damn it." Mason ran his fingers though his hair. "It's not that simple."

"Sure it is. You've found her." Hawk grinned. "Never thought you'd be first though. Always figured Dane would succumb to the lure of love first."

"Hey," Dane said, in protest. "I fall in and out of love weekly."

It was true of most of them. But for Dane, the romantic in him saw the good in everyone – until he saw the great in the next one.

"He's right there." Swede smacked him on the shoulder.

The group fell silent as two stretchers carefully brought out their fallen comrades. A reminder of how precious life really was.

CHAPTER 14

WORDS TO LIVE by. She did have this. And she really appreciated them. It had helped to right her world. As had his kiss. Stupid really.

After being unloaded, she was taken through to a large medical facility where she was carefully moved to an examining bed. She was treated so carefully she had to wonder if Mason's warning to the medics hadn't preceded her.

Once on the bed, her feet were carefully unwrapped, her wrist checked – and she'd forgotten about the chafing and bruising brought on by the restraints Daniel had put on her. She studied them critically then dismissed them. Torn skin, green discoloration and tenderness. All mild compared to her feet. Her injection site had even calmed down. Now that she was being treated, and warm, she was exhausted. Had it only been last night she'd had a fever. Did they know?

Did any of it matter?

She lay quiet as the muttering rolled around her. Her feet were a concern. Duh. She knew that too. A smidgeon of fear rippled through her as they continued to stay at her feet.

"I know they aren't the best, but surely they don't warrant that kind of attention," she said to them.

The men looked over their glasses at her. "You've run them

raw."

"I remember." And how. She lay back down and let them mutter. As long as her running through the bush days were done, she was fine.

"We're going to need to clean them well, and we'll be able to see the damage a little clearer."

At the term clean, she bolted upright again. "Mason cleaned and bandaged them already."

The one doctor walked over to her. He laid a restraining hand on her shoulder. "Please lie down and relax."

She flopped backwards and groaned. "I'd really like to go home."

"Not today," she was firmly told.

"Tomorrow?" she asked hopefully.

And all she received were multiple head shakes.

The same doctor said, "It's far too early to make that decision. You will need to be debriefed."

Right. Military talk for someone wanted to talk to her. Of course. She wasn't going anywhere any time soon. Then again that also meant she might see Mason again. Possibly more than once. He said he'd find her.

She had to trust he would.

In the meantime they were going to take care of her whether she liked it or not. A nurse came over with a bowl of warm water.

She lost her smile. Damn, this was going to hurt. Another nurse brought a foot bath and helped her sit up. Slipping her feet into the warm water, she groaned gently as soothing warmth eased through her puffy skin.

"Does that feel good?"

"It feels lovely."

She sat there for several long minutes loving the treatment. By the time her feet were cleaned, they were on fire again, and she wished she could go put them back into the water. Just when she was at the point of requesting a second foot bath, the nurse put on something that numbed the pain. It gave her feet an instant cooling effect that had her resting back. "Thank you. That feels better."

"We do try to help," the nurse said with a bright smile that matched the rest of her.

Done, Tesla lay back down, quietly relieved the ordeal was over. She hadn't expected to nap, but warm and safe had the same effect as a sleeping pill and she drifted in and out. She woke when there were sounds of someone coming in to her room. She sat up, wiping the sleep out of her eyes and looked around.

"Feel better?"

Mason. With a bright smile, she shifted so she could see him.

"Easy, you don't have to move." He walked around the side and sat on the edge of the bed. He reached out and picked up her hand. "You look rested. Do you feel better?"

Looking at their joined hands, she realized how nice a man he really was. He was so damn nice.

"Did they take care of your feet?" he prodded her when she didn't answer.

She winced at the reminder. "Yes."

He laughed. "It's over. That's all that matters."

"And now I'm starving." She frowned. "When does anyone eat around here? It's been hours."

Now he was grinning. "I actually have permission to take you out of here."

She gasped. "Really? Oh, let's go."

He pointed to the wheelchair she hadn't noticed sitting at the doorway. "In that."

Her face fell.

"It's the only way."

She glared at it. Then at him. "Fine."

His grin was a mile wide as she reached up her arms to wrap around his neck. He scooped her up and carried her to the chair. She sat down and wiggled into a better position. He stepped behind her and grabbed the handles, pushing her out of the room.

"Where are we going?"

"Outside to the garden."

"Lovely." And she meant it. "It is a beautiful afternoon."

He pushed out the front door to a small garden on the side. In the sunshine, she tilted her face upward.

"When are you leaving?" she asked, knowing he'd come to say good-bye. His silence was too silent. As if he didn't know what to say.

"Tomorrow."

"So soon?"

"Yes."

She nodded. "Good. You like to be busy."

"We have to go after the men who attacked you."

She twisted to look up to him. "Really? But that's dangerous."

He laughed. "And that's why we go, so the world is safer for everyone else."

"Of course." She leaned her head back, already missing him. Yet they were nothing other than friends and even that was in doubt. They had nothing in a relationship...and yet they had something. But what? She didn't know what to say. "How long are you going to be gone?"

"A week." But it was too fast an answer. He either didn't want to tell her the truth or he didn't know.

"Or a month?"

"No. It won't be that long."

"Good. There are a lot of bad guys out there. You can't spend too much time with just one of them."

He walked around and squatted down in front of her. "True enough. I'm in high demand."

"Ha." She scoffed with a teasing grin. "You just think so."

After that the conversation turned to a casual discussion as they both tried to avoid any reference to their relationship. They talked about nothing and everything and all superficial. Before too long he stood up. "I've got to go."

She swallowed hard but nodded bravely. "I understand."

"I'll take you back to your room."

She wanted to tell him to leave her where she was. That she'd sit in the sun a little longer. Only she didn't think she could make it back on her own steam. Just the effort of not talking to him like she wanted to was exhausting. He turned her around and pushed her forward. Before she was ready, they were back. He scooped her up and sat her down on the bed. He opened his mouth as if to say something and then stopped.

"What?"

He shook his head. "It doesn't matter."

She frowned. It did matter, but he wasn't going to be persuaded otherwise. "Fine. Keep your secrets."

"No secrets. Just thoughts I can't do anything about right now."

Okay. Good enough. "Will you call me when you get home?"

He nodded. "Are you going to be here? Or will you be back into your own home?"

"I could hope so. I'm here for the presentation and demonstration. They were bringing me to Coronado when I was taken. I'll be six months integrating the software – at least." She shrugged. "It's not a done deal yet, though the powers that be were acting like it was. If it goes through, I'll be moving here until the system is set up."

His eyebrows shot up. "Really?"

She nodded. "Didn't you know? That's when I was kidnapped – on the trip here."

"No. Somehow I didn't." They stared at each other in bemusement. "I knew you were travelling but not why."

"Does it matter," she whispered.

"Maybe not, but…"

He sounded distracted as if this was new information, and he didn't know how to integrate it with the old. She patted his hand. "I'm sure they've already figured it out."

But he didn't sound convinced. She studied him. "You should know if you're hunting them."

He gave a curt nod. "I'm going to leave now."

"Oh," she said in a small voice.

"It's time."

She nodded and swallowed. "Well, it was nice to see you."

"I couldn't walk away without saying good-bye."

"Thank you." As he walked to the door, she called out, "Say good-bye to the others."

He nodded and gave her a small wave.

SHE LOOKED SO damn lost in the hospital bed. As if he was leaving her. Which he was. Damn. He strode back and picked her up. This time he kissed her like he wanted to. He kissed her like he'd been wanting to do since he'd first seen her. He poured all the heat and longing he could pour into the simple movement. He pulled back, lay her back down on the bed, leaned over and kissed her briefly on the temple. "I'll be back."

"Hurry," she whispered.

He closed his eyes, then turned and strode out, his mind consumed with tidbits she'd dropped on him.

Damn it. He walked into the conference room twenty minutes later. He had a meeting with the team. And he had a few questions he needed answered. Like why hadn't they known Tesla was moving to the base at least temporarily and had been kidnapped on the way. How many people knew what was happening? How many people had she told? In theory, her family and friends. Anyone else? She had her own company – so everyone in her company? It was a place to start. The question was, had anyone done that leg work?

Swede waited for him.

"How is she?"

"Holding. I took her out in the garden for a bit of fresh air."

Swede nodded. "She'd have liked that."

"She did. But…" he stopped and looked at Swede. "Did you know what she was doing when she was kidnapped?"

"No. I don't think we were ever told?"

Mason explained.

Swede's face darkened. "Now that would be an interesting

chain to yank."

"It would, but we're on our way to go after the men who kidnapped her."

"And the person who set her up?"

Mason's gaze narrowed. "That's the trick, isn't it – he's still at large."

"And still available to go after Tesla."

CHAPTER 15

A week later

THE DAYS PASSED slowly. She'd told the authorities everything she could remember. And they'd come back day after day and asked her more questions.

She had nothing more to add. She had a small condo for her use close by, and she was mobile now but definitely not back to normal. So her life was all about getting back to work and healing. Walking was much easier, although running was still out of the question.

She walked out to the small patio that was part of her new home. It was tiny, brick and quaint. But it was hers for the moment, and she felt safe here. Surrounded by other military families. For the millionth time she wondered where Mason was. What he and the rest of the team were doing. And how successful was their trip. Had they caught the guys that were after her? Was she safe? Or were the men still at large?

Mason was always on her mind. Yet he wasn't hers. But he could be. If she wanted, he could be. Maybe.

Did she want that? He was a hero. His career was dangerous. Like Harry's. He could die like Harry had died.

Tears came to her eyes.

She swiped at them impatiently. She'd rather have loved and

lost Harry than not have had him in her life at all. Love was like that. And she'd go through the loss all over again if it meant having the joyful memories of being with him in the first place. She'd take as many of those years as she could have. And the same for Mason. She'd still hold close any memories she had. The choices weren't great but to have spent time with him, loving him... well that was special. Sure it would be nice if he were in a nice safe job like a computer programmer but then he would be Mason...

There were no guarantees in life. Look at the nightmare she'd been through already this last week. If Mason's team hadn't saved her...

Now it seemed like all she did was wait for Mason to show up again.

At least her work was going well. She was almost done with the last set of tweaks. Was all set to give her demonstration tomorrow. Combine that to almost being healed, then life was good.

Her phone rang. But of course she'd left it on the computer table. She walked back inside. She checked the number but didn't recognize it. She knew better than to respond to any unusual calls. Although her phone was being monitored while here, and security was constantly on the prowl. At night time they were outside her house. In the day time they were around, she just never knew who they were.

And that meant there was no point in looking but of course she couldn't stop herself. She'd wondered if the gardener that seemed to do daily rounds was one of them. He'd done her yard and her neighbors then a day later she'd seen him on the side of the road.

It did make her feel better knowing someone was out there.

She returned to her work. The presentation needed a little tweaking then she should be good there too. Her staff were more keyed up over this than she was. Of course she'd promised them a bonus if she managed to pull it off.

The government had a lot of money for her type of software. She'd love to be financially stable, to be able to give it to them free, but no such luck so she was looking for a fair price. Lower than market value as the value had gone up. Her manager had been contacted any number of times in the last few days about her program. All calls had been forwarded to the government.

There was no way in hell she'd sell out her government. It wasn't possible for her to do that to her brother. Mason. The others.

Too bad she was so damn tired. Another cup of coffee then she'd be done.

After pouring the coffee into the cup, she walked back to the computer. There were several chat messages from one of her staff. She started answering.

By the time she was done, her coffee was almost cold. She stood up and walked back to the kitchen. The pot was empty. Damn.

She rinsed out her cup and took a sip of water instead. As she stared out the window, she caught sight of the freshly mowed lawn. Good. She loved sitting out there in the evenings.

Turning around she gasped. Shrieked. And dropped her cup.

Two men dressed in black jumped her. She fought like a wildcat until the sting of a needle filled her veins with an icy liquid.

She collapsed unconscious into their arms.

"HEY, MASON, HOW'D the mission go?"

The black look on Mason's face should have given the young man the answer. In fact, it should have sent the man running in the opposite direction. Instead the man stood, ready to ask more questions.

He muttered to Swede, "I must be losing my edge."

"You're in love, it's allowed."

Without missing a stride he reached out and punched Swede in his rock hard gut.

Swede gave a snort. "Damn mosquitos."

A soldier raced toward them. "Mason."

Mason groaned. "Damn it. I wanted a shower, was that too much to ask?"

The soldier reached them. "The commander is looking for you." He lowered his voice. "Now, I'm not supposed to say anything, but it's to do with that lady you rescued."

Mason froze. Then he was sprinting to the commander's office. He burst through the door completely ignoring protocol. "Tell me Tesla's okay."

The commander glared at him. "She's missing. Gear up."

Swede stood behind him. "We're ready."

"How the hell…" Mason was at a loss for words. How could they lose this woman again?

"We think two men posing as her company employees walked into the house and left about an hour later."

"With her?"

The commander rubbed the back of his head. "She was under surveillance. Both men were knocked out cold, and as we can't find her, we're assuming yes."

"The cameras?"

"At the garage, yes," he nodded.

"A large SUV. Yes, we've checked the plates. They are ours." He stood up and glared at them. "She was due at a reception tonight and her presentation was the main event. Then she was going to be doing a demonstration tomorrow morning."

"Her house?" Mason barked.

"Searched and clean."

"No one knows anything?" Mason was beside himself. They had to know what direction she'd gone. They needed information. And they needed it now.

"There is one thing," the commander said. "When they were searching her house her laptop was gone, but her coworkers had an instant messaging system on her tablet. She answered the chat the last time just over an hour ago."

"Were they talking to her since?"

"Yes, but she didn't respond." He looked down at the papers on his desk. "We're presuming she couldn't."

"We need to know what direction they've taken."

"We're tracking the SUV now. It's heading south out of the city. We're on it."

"Any cameras confirm she's inside as it could be a decoy."

"We can't confirm that at this time."

Mason nodded, his fists clenching and releasing. "I need to see her place."

The commander said, "They are waiting for you. You know how much we need this software. And given the type of software, we can't let it get into enemy hands."

Mason glared at him. "Tesla is not expendable."

He turned on his heel and raced out. Swede behind him. The others were waiting outside. While Swede filled them in, Mason found a truck. They had to find Tesla. And fast.

CHAPTER 16

THE VEHICLE DROVE steadily, the rhythmic movement keeping her in a half hypnotic trance. She'd woken in a stupor with her mind struggling to make sense of what happened. When she figured it out, her body was too paralyzed to do anything about it.

"How is our guest?" someone asked up front. "Is she still asleep?"

"She's asleep."

"Good. We can't lose her."

"Maybe not, but she needs to pay for what she did to my brother."

"That's not for us to do." The first man snapped. "We hand her and her computer over and we get paid. It's simple."

"For you, it's simple. You don't care that they caught you and left you behind."

The first man sniggered. "That's funny."

"There's nothing funny about it. Besides, I didn't stay caught. Sometimes you need to play possum to come out the winner."

"Ha, you weren't playing possum. You're just damn lucky we found you in time. You were grandstanding. Playing the big ego role. He was your friend and you beat him. Only you didn't.

He turned the tables and caught you."

"And like the game it is, I turned the tables yet again and escaped."

Finally, Tesla understood. One of the men was Daniel. The man who'd held her captive in the cabin. The man Mason had said he'd taken care of, but when the others went to pick him up, he'd disappeared. Daniel had been behind everything. She didn't know who or why this man was here. She'd understood he was doing this for a paycheck, a point she really hated him for, but she wasn't surprised. There were many other men like him out there.

It was who was paying him that she wanted caught. Daniel was just a soldier.

It had occurred to her that there were few people who could know where she was now. Less than the fingers on her right hand. Making them all suspects now that she'd been kidnapped yet again.

God, that just pissed her off.

How could she have been so stupid? Or how could her guards be so stupid. Hell, maybe the lawn mower guy did just mow lawns. Did anyone know she was missing yet?

Her staff would know. How long before they raised the alarm? She often power napped on them when they were pulling late nights. Her computer would shut down within minutes of her last stroke on the keyboard. A security precaution. And nothing was held in any one place on purpose. The program couldn't be stolen that way.

But her computer lay in the footwell beside her. These men were serious and she was in deep trouble.

That same anger at being stupid enough to get kidnapped

was firing again. This time at Mason.

He just had to go away and leave her alone.

Now look what had happened?

The vehicle slowed and turned off the main highway. She closed her eyes and started calling mentally to Mason. *Where are you Mason? I need you. Please. Please find me.*

"Hey look, she's awake."

"Not good. We're pulling in for gas. Make sure she doesn't create a disturbance."

"Oh, she's not going to say anything, are you, darling?"

She opened her eyes. And the biggest ugliest man in the world stared down at her, just hoping she'd make a wrong move. She shook her head.

Hell no, she wasn't going to go up against this stranger.

But she knew Mason would.

Just as soon as he got here.

MASON DROVE THE SUV. The vehicle that supposedly held Tesla had been spotted heading south. That didn't mean they didn't have plans to go to a different destination, but they had a direction to start.

They also had no proof that Tesla was in that vehicle. She could be anywhere by now. Why now? Because of her presentation tonight? If she gave it, everyone would know what the program could do. And that was something they didn't want advertised. Then again, she'd be under tight security while there. She should have been under the best freakin' security while he was gone. She should have had someone living in the damn house with her.

He understood there were men outside watching, but somehow she'd been taken anyway. So how did that help?

He wandered through her small house. He could so see her sitting there at her computer and working away. Intent on saving the world one soldier at a time. But that didn't mean there weren't clues here.

She was back on her feet and mobile, if a bit slow.

Slow was good. She'd take better care if she was slow. He saw her socks off to one side. And one slipper off to the other. Was she barefoot again? That wouldn't be good.

"She'd have left a message if she could," Swede remarked. "She's resilient. She'll make it through this."

Mason nodded. She would. He'd see to it. He walked over to the office. The techs were working on her desk, but her laptop was missing. The enemy had it.

After all, they were hoping for the program. "Where is the program she was working on?" he asked the techs suddenly.

The man shrugged. "I have no idea. Above my pay grade."

"Right." Likely above everyone's in the room.

So who would know and who had access to it? If it was Tesla alone, then they were in trouble. If it was Tesla and someone else's then that person needed help to access it. And if it was both of them together then the enemy would need both to get access. How smart was Tesla? Had she managed to hide the system from everyone else but herself? Leaving her in the ultimate position and therefore the easiest torture to get what they wanted? Or was she one of many working on small pieces of the program that would come together at the end.

And it could still be broken in less than two hours.

She'd seemed pretty sure that no one could get it from her.

So she must have something up her sleeve.

However, what about the others who worked for her?

Did they have access? And if they did, were they being pro-tected?

"We need to find the rest of her staff," he said to Swede. "Pick them up before anyone else does."

"You think they need to be present for the enemy to gain access to the program?"

"Or to use as a way to torture Tesla. She might withstand the torture they throw at her, but she would give in if they tortured her friends."

Hawk spat on the ground. "True. So let's snag them so they have less leverage."

"And her father."

Swede grimaced. "Good luck with that. He's already here and raising Cain. He wants to talk to you as soon as possible."

"Why me?"

"You led the last mission that rescued her."

So maybe it couldn't be that bad to speak with him. Harry had said he'd been hell to have as a parent, but...surely as both Harry and Tesla turned out to be great, he couldn't be that bad.

It was way worse.

Her father was a retired Marine, a SEAL of course. And that was evident from the moment Mason walked in. His team was standing outside. He wasn't sure if they were here for support or to share in any accolades. He could tell from the first moment that there weren't going to be any of those. This man was ferocious.

"Lieutenant Mason Hunter?"

Mason nodded.

"Where the hell is my daughter?"

He opened his mouth to answer then realized he had nothing to say. "I don't know, sir."

"And why don't you know, Lieutenant?"

"We haven't found her yet, sir."

"And yet you're sitting here doing nothing. Are you not?"

"No, sir."

"What exactly are you doing?"

"Searching for her through the videos, preparing to pick up her coworkers, and her house is currently being taken apart to see if there are any clues to her whereabouts, sir."

The man straightened, appearing much taller than his already overwhelming six foot four build. He might be Tesla's father, but he was still military. And Mason realized that he'd have been a hell of a leader. Maybe Mason had missed out on an opportunity to serve under him. He looked like he'd raise a whole lot of hell to get the job done.

"And my daughter, are these men going to hurt her, Lieutenant?"

He hesitated. The man might be a retired SEAL, but he was still a father.

"The truth, Officer."

Mason nodded. "Yes, I believe they will."

"Then you'd better get her before that happens, hadn't you?"

There wasn't much he could say because he'd do his damnedest, but after losing her the last time these guy weren't likely to make the same mistake again. She'd be either securely trussed and likely to one of them, or she'd be unconscious or drugged. Any and all resistance kept to a minimum. He should know as he'd employed the same tactics himself. All that he could do was find her before they broke her spirit. For hurting her in anyway, they'd pay. He could just hope it wouldn't be worse than a few scars.

But he knew men like this. If they wanted to, they'd carve her while still alive and eat her for lunch.

"Sir, if at all possible, I'll bring your daughter back." Mason saluted and turned to leave. At the doorway, he could see Swede and the others a little way away.

Tesla's father called out, "Lieutenant."

Mason turned.

"Are you bringing her back for my sake, your sake, or both?"

The merest of an expression crossed his features, but Tesla's father caught it. He gave a mirthless smirk. "Right. Then you'd better get moving before you disappoint both of us."

"It's not you or myself that I'm worried about disappointing," Mason returned smartly. "It is and always has been to avoid disappointing Tesla. Your daughter is a fine woman, doing a wonderful thing. I will do my best for her sake regardless."

And he gave the briefest of nods and retreated.

After all, in this case it was the best defense.

CHAPTER 17

THE MILES CARRIED on forever. She had to go to the bathroom and soon was going to pee in the damn car. What the hell did they expect? She'd been trussed up like a turkey for hours. She'd done her part and had kept quiet the whole time. Well, it was time for that to change.

"I need to go to the bathroom," she called out.

There was a spat of guttural mutterings then the vehicle slowed. She watched as shiny lights kicked in overhead showing a gas station. She was happy with that. Anything to relieve her bladder. They pulled around to the back. One of the men got out and disappeared. Daniel crawled to the back of the vehicle. "If you do anything stupid, call or try to make a run for it..." he threatened.

"I know. You'll make me pay," she said wearily. "Yes, you've told me several times already."

He just glared at her. The back door of the SUV suddenly popped open and the second man stood grinning down at her, and she realized he was planning on coming into the bathroom with her. Oh shit.

"Just so you know that if you hurt me, I won't be worth as much," she said, hoping to convince them to leave her alone.

"Ha. As long as you're alive, you're worth a lot." Daniel

smirked.

"But if I'm not capable of working then the buyer won't be happy," she snapped. "And I'll be happy to tell him why I'm hurt."

The two men exchanged glances, but the hands that reached for her were gentler than any she'd felt from them up until now. In other words, they were scared of their boss. Good thing. And she was pretty sure Daniel was an old friend of Mason's. Or maybe friend wasn't quite the word. But she could identify him and if he cared about that, he wasn't showing it. The other guy she tried to get a decent description of, but what the hell. How was Mason going to find a medium height, medium build, medium brown hair asshole like this one? Of course the huge hooked nose and gut helped make him unique. The busted teeth might help as well. She didn't want anything to do with that.

Daniel might be a mercenary, but she didn't get the idea he got off on hurting women. His asshole partner, now that was a different story.

He hated women. Too many women probably turned him down on dates while he was growing up. They probably knew then he was trouble.

The scary asshole held her arm in a death grip as she walked to the small bathroom around the side of the large building. She'd love to run screaming inside, but she had no idea what they'd do.

"See that pregnant woman walking around the vehicle waiting for her husband to fill up the car?"

She nodded, her stomach sinking.

"Any funny stuff from you and she gets the first bullet. Right in the belly."

Yeah, he got off on hurting women.

"Understand?"

She nodded. "Yes."

"Good." He unlocked the bathroom, stuck his head inside, nodded then shoved her in. "Hurry up."

And he locked the door behind her.

Shit. He'd left her hands tied up. Crap. She sat down on the floor and ran her arms and the rope under her bum so she could slip her legs through and stand up with her hands now in front of her. Much better. She dropped her pants and relieved herself while her mind raced in a million directions looking for answers. She had to leave a message. Something of some kind. But if they came in and saw it then the poor woman outside was going to die.

So what options did she have?

Not to mention she had no pen or pencil and no way to write a message that would be hidden from someone using the bathroom and not the scary dude.

Then she got it. Her wrists were raw already so she used her teeth to make one bleed a little more freely, then sitting on the toilet she wrote the message at her feet. Only to be seen by someone sitting down and likely not noticed from the door as the linoleum floor was a mottle brown.

After she finished, she flushed the toilet and ran to the sink. She quickly washed her hands and grabbed and extra bit of paper towel to staunch the bleeding, but it was already slowing so all was good.

The door opened suddenly and it was the scary dude looking at her.

She mustered a smile. "Good timing, I'm done."

His face fell as if he'd hoped to catch her sitting on the toilet. Sick bastard.

Without saying a word he led her back to the vehicle. Once there, he gave a surreptitious glance around, and ordered, "Get in."

She stared at the back of the SUV and groaned. "Why can't I sit in the seat like a normal passenger?"

"Shut the fuck up and get in," he snarled.

So much for that. She glanced around, but no one appeared to be in a position to see the single female get into the back of the SUV. Too damn bad. Someone might see her and call it in. And she'd gotten a message out. Maybe someone would see that.

It did give her a little bit of hope. And she'd take all of the hope she could get.

Once inside, she tried to listen to the two men as they talked. She was hoping to hear a location, a name, some sign of direction as to their destination. So far nothing.

"Where are we going?" she called out.

Silence.

Then the scary dude yelled back. "None of your business."

"Really, well it is my business as that's where you're taking me. If I wasn't involved in your stupid deals then it wouldn't involve me but as I am…"

She didn't know where the bravado came from – maybe the thought that someone might finally see the message was helping. Bolstering her confidence.

Only she smelt his breath first. Then felt the blow that came out of nowhere.

She blacked out.

THE ENEMY VEHICLE had been spotted heading toward the Mexican border. It could turn off before hitting that checkpoint, but at least Mason had a direction to start. They'd receive live updates as they got them. They also had no proof that Tesla was in that vehicle.

That bothered him more than anything.

He and the team were getting ready to board a plane to a point just past where the vehicle was assumed to be headed. They were due to fly out in ten minutes. Ten of the longest damn minutes he'd felt in forever. What the fuck was taking so damn long?

"Easy, Mason. We're leaving in a couple of minutes."

"A couple of minutes she doesn't have."

A gas station attendant had called the police to say a number had been left written in blood in the washroom. The cops called the number and got Mason. It was his cell number. He had no idea how Tesla got the number but she was brilliant in anything tech so it was no surprise. Better yet, it was the first real confirmation that Tesla was indeed in the vehicle they were tracking.

Now the team was geared for war. They might be fighting in their own country, but it was going to be lethal nonetheless. If Tesla was taken across the line, well they'd be heading down there too. There was no place in this world they wouldn't go to do what needed to be done.

"Mexico doesn't make much sense," Hawk said. "Unless they are meeting someone who will take them overseas."

"That's possible. The Mexican authorities aren't going to care except if the money crossing their hands isn't quite enough."

"Which is an easy fix for these guys. We need to find them before they cross, or we could lose her."

"Not going to happen." Mason jumped to his feet and raced to get on the plane. Before he got halfway, he heard the engines start up in preparation.

"Damn good thing," he muttered.

The time was short. The distance difficult. And the timing – everything.

The military plane was in the air within seconds. It would be a short flight so no one had a chance to relax. They set up a strategy as soon as they landed. Nothing else was possible.

"Take it easy, Mason," Dane said. "You're going to need to calm down or you'll scare the hell out of her."

Hawk laughed. "Have you looked at that girl? She doesn't scare easily."

"No, she doesn't. But everyone, especially those not trained like we are, have their breaking point. She's going to hit it at some point."

Mason nodded. "She will. But it won't be today."

The others grinned.

"So did you decide," Swede asked, a big grin on his face.

"No." Mason snapped. "But she's not for you."

"She just needs a chance to see me without you around," the big man said. "Besides, once she gets to know me, she'll love me."

"Just like all the other women," Hawk teased. "I'm sure you say that about them all."

"Hell no," Swede said. "She's different."

"She is. She's honorable. Trustworthy. Stubborn," Shadow said. "I admire her. What she's doing and how she's faced all this torment so far. I love that she was still going strong on her project instead of letting the pressure cause her to back off."

"I have to admit to having been worried about that myself," Mason admitted. "But once she healed enough, she's supposedly been working sixteen hour days on her project."

"And now the demonstration is tomorrow and the presentation is tonight. And she's not going to make it."

Mason growled. "She's going to make it. Not tonight. But she'll be there, ready and capable of giving her demonstration by ten in the morning, or I'll know the reason why."

His comment was more than an order. It was a request that the men give their all to make this happen. That no matter what, they'd get Tesla back at the base to give that very important demonstration. There were too many lives at stake. Tesla's was one of them. But he'd spent way too many days in combat boots to not understand the advantage her software could give them. And she was a genius. If she'd been able to do what she said she'd done, he knew she could take this level and shoot it up so much higher. She was gifted. And dedicated.

Had Harry known?

Mason could wish he knew how well Tesla had done now. What she'd been motivated to do in the wake of Harry's death? Did her father even understand? Or did he not appreciate a daughter still alive when his son had died?

One never knew. The world of parenting being one he'd avoided all his life. He had been an only child, his parents dying when he was just a child. He'd been raised by his aunt and uncle and he'd had a good life, enough he hadn't craved that need to be loved. If anything he wanted something like they had. A long time relationship with someone who understood. Given his profession, the number of failed marriages amongst the veterans after they came home from the wars, the violence he dealt with every day…he was just damn happy to be almost normal himself.

He couldn't imagine finding someone else that would appreciate who and what he was at this point in his life. Better to love and leave them.

Right?

Sure, his head said. *As long as we're not talking about Tesla.*

CHAPTER 18

MINDLESS AND IN pain from the uncomfortable position, Tesla lay almost comatose in the back.

The vehicle swerved violently to the side, hitting the shoulder before being reefed back out to the road again.

She moaned as she bounced forward, smashing the back of the seats and then down to the other side as the vehicle swerved across the road. Luckily with her hands in front, she could brace herself slightly.

"Who the fuck is that?" Daniel screamed in frustration as he struggled to keep the big vehicle on the road. "Fucking idiot drivers."

Tesla cheered. They needed a few more drivers like that. It woke Daniel and his nasty partner up. And her. She was more alert now.

Was that a good thing? Still, just knowing that her kidnappers had been shaken was good enough for her. She'd started to wonder if anything could rattle them.

And where was Mason now? He should be tracking her. He wouldn't leave her to her fate. Even if she'd upset him. Had she upset him? That badly? She hoped not. She wanted that idiot driver vehicle to be them, but it wasn't likely. Just then the SUV slowed down and took a sharp right. And hit rough road. She moaned as her sore shoulders were jostled and bounced. She had no control as the big rig carried her further away from Mason.

Hot tears clung to her eyes. And she shuddered. She was going to give him a piece of her mind for this. He'd said she was safe.

He'd lied to her. Her rational mind knew that he was not responsible, but she wanted someone to *be* responsible, and Mason was the one who came to mind. Hell, he was always the one who came to mind. He was too damn beautiful. No guy should be so gorgeous. And of course that was reason enough to have nothing to do with him. Get rid of him before he got rid of her with a prettier model. She was fine, but there was nothing special or unique about her. She was all about average. And in this world average sucked.

Brush banged against the side of the SUV, filling the back window with dark shadows. The air inside tensed. Was there something wrong?

Please let there be something wrong. She desperately needed there to be something to disrupt their plans. A chill had settled on her skin as she realized a turn off the highway meant they were coming to their intended destination. And a hidden one at that.

She was running out of time.

"They aren't here yet?" Daniel's worried voice filtered to the back.

"They should be. Although we made good time. We're actually a little early."

"Not that early."

She heard Daniel swear as he pulled the vehicle to a stop.

"Is this the right location?"

"According to the GPS, it is."

"There's no way a plane is going to land on this strip."

"Bush planes land in all sorts of places," Daniel said. "It's a proper runway, just rundown and overgrown with weeds."

"Good thing I'm not going. I doubt any plane could take off here."

"Oh, you're going all right. That was the deal."

"Except we didn't pick up Charlie. He was supposed to take the rig back. Now that's left to me."

Tesla could hear Daniel's muttering under his breath but not a resolution. If she was up against only one man, even a mercenary like Daniel, she'd have a much better chance than if she were up against the scary dude as well. But she wasn't going to be able to ditch him until she was on the plane. And that was really bad news.

The men got out of the truck. She expected them to come around and haul her out but sounds faded as they walked further away. She struggled to her knees and looked around. With her hands in front of her, it was easier to twist around and look out the window. As far as she could see, there was nothing but trees and more trees. There had to be something. They spoke of a runway. Surely that was here somewhere. Except as she studied the area outside the vehicle, there was no sign of the men.

There wasn't going to be a better time. She opened the back door as quietly as she could, and pushing it open just enough that she could slip out, she bent down and crept to the closest tree. Then the next one and the next one.

When she didn't hear a mad shout behind her, she flat out ran. She kept the tracks in sight, knowing she'd end up lost if she didn't, while yet trying to stay hidden. Following the tracks would be easier, but they'd also have an easier time of tracking her down too. She didn't dare get caught. Unless it was by her SEAL.

She almost giggled at that.

A SEAL to the rescue. Or he would be if he actually got here and rescued her.

Thank God her feet were mostly better. And that the ass-holes had grabbed her shoes and jacket. She was in a better position now than ever. Well, almost. Unfortunately, her jacket was too bright to keep her hidden in the brush. The neon yellow reflective stripes did their job well. It helped others to see her. And so not what she wanted right now.

She grabbed it by the waist and pulled it over her head. Off her back but now wrapped around her restraints. Still, inside out kept the reflective strips hidden.

She gasped for breath, struggling to find her natural stride. At home she used to jog every morning. Then that was before the kidnapping. This last week of healing had helped her feet, but they were not up for a twenty mile sprint. She breathed through her nose, tried to massage the stitch in her side. A stitch was deadly to a runner. She tried to take long slow breaths and find that natural rhythm. She lengthened her stride and dodged around a tree and up a small hollow. She shifted around rocks and headed down an easier pathway. She was still running parallel to the road. She had no idea how far away the main highway was, but she wanted to reach it fast. She'd still have to flag someone down and get help, but she'd take her chances with a stranger over these two men.

She could hear a vehicle approaching ahead. She slipped into a thick stand of brush and caught her breath. The black SUV raced down past her. It never slowed. She shivered. Thank God.

However, it also meant they were ahead of her and could be waiting up ahead. That was dangerous. She had to see them first and she was running toward them.

Damn it. What if they were out of the vehicle and running toward her?

She didn't know what to do. If she did nothing, she'd be sitting there until dark and chances were good she'd get lost for real. They could just sit there in the dark and wait until she showed up on the main highway.

Then what was she going to do?

Stilled by indecision, she froze as she heard another vehicle. What was she going to do? She cocked an ear, trying to see who else was arriving. Instead, the sound approached and disappeared without her seeing it. Then she got it. The vehicles were on the highway.

She slipped out of her spot. And crept forward to the next grove. There were a lot of hiding places and she moved carefully. There was no sign of the SUV. Or any other vehicles. So now what? She could walk parallel to the road, staying in the shadows, or she could stay and let Mason find her.

Damn it. Which way to go?

"THAT'S DANIEL." MASON swore as he caught a glimpse of his archenemy whipping past. Mason turned the vehicle around and ripped down the road after the SUV. The road was curvy and the SUV seemed to be always just that little ahead. He gunned the motor.

The plan to get ahead had worked, but he only just realized

how well. What was the chance Tesla had been right there within twenty feet of him? He hadn't expected to see them within minutes of hitting the road.

"Keep an eye out."

"That had to be her," Hawk said. "It's the same license plate."

"I recognized Daniel." Mason swore again. "I should have killed him before."

"Yep, you should have," Swede agreed.

"I'd hoped to get more information from him. Pick him up on the way back so we can stop these attacks on Tesla. She has to be safe."

But the SUV was gone from sight. He pushed the vehicle as fast as it would go. They had to be ahead of them still.

Unless they'd taken a turn off.

"So far she's been nothing but in trouble," Hawk said. "I can't imagine her safe. It seems too preposterous."

"We'll find her." Mason searched the road, but there were no signs of anyone. Or any vehicle. No sign of a pedestrian or wildlife even. "Where the hell are they? We should have seen them by now."

"Unless they left the highway somewhere and we missed it."

Mason considered that information for a quick second then hit the brake – hard. The SUV came to a bone shuddering stop. He made a quick change of direction and started back the way he'd come – at half speed. "If that's the case, we need to look for any signs of where they'd have turned off the road."

"There…" Hawk pointed to the left. "Back up, back up."

Mason hit the brakes, shifted into reverse and backed up, tires squealing.

He saw it then. He pulled off the road onto the tracks and stopped.

"We'll continue on foot. We've blocked the trail, so they aren't going to be able to leave this way. The ground is soft, wet. We should be able to track them easily enough."

Mason smiled. "Good."

He pulled slightly forward until he found a place where the road diverged. Take the road less travelled, and he parked. "That will do it."

The men got out. After a quick check over their firepower and ammo situation, Mason took the lead. The others spread out. Now to find Tesla.

They moved forward in a steady encircling ring like a noose tightening on the enemy's head. There was no sign of anyone. And no sign of anyone having passed.

An odd sound came from the left, more of a whisper of a sound. He didn't recognize it. And that made it very interesting. He slipped off of the side and came around behind the noise. And frowned. There was the SUV, but it appeared to be empty. This was the old airstrip, but it didn't look to have seen any maintenance in the last many years. Hell, from a decade at least. They were going to land a plane here? Take her out that way? That was taking a chance.

So what had gone wrong?

Besides Tesla?

And where was she?

He cocked his ear. There was someone now running. He grinned. She still favored her sore feet. He'd recognize those footsteps anywhere.

He signaled to the others and took off after her.

She was running at a great clip. He was amazed. But she still wasn't going to get away from him. He hadn't come all this way to lose her now.

And yet…he lost her. He strode forward listening, his eyes glued to the trail she'd left behind. They were almost to the highway. But they were on the wrong side of where his SUV should be.

He wanted to call out to her but couldn't take the chance.

He closed his eyes and imitated Hawk's bird cry. She might recognize it.

After sending the second cry he crept forward again.

He turned, looking for her, and realized she'd slipped from the back grove to the next stand of trees. He grinned. She'd done well. He needed her to keep that up. To keep her spirit up.

With a quick glance around he made his move and crept up to her.

He quickly wrapped an arm around her ribs, slapping his other hand over her mouth to stop her from crying out.

"Shh. It's me, Mason."

CHAPTER 19

TESLA CRIED OUT, but no sound erupted as a hand had clapped over her mouth. Strong arms held her. Instinct said to run. Instinct said to fight. But her heart said she was safe. Then his words filled her ears and she understood. It was Mason. She sagged in place, her knees weak and her spine suddenly boneless.

He'd come for her.

He spun her around until he looked down at her. "Are you okay," he whispered in a hoarse guttural tone. "Did they hurt you?"

She clasped her hands on either side of his head and shook her head wildly. "No, they didn't hurt me. They didn't have time. You came, oh thank God."

"Are you sure you're okay."

"I'm fine. I'm so glad to see you."

"Shh, it's okay. Be quiet. Shh. Be quiet."

She tried. Honest she did, but it was so freakin' hard. She finally looped her arms around his neck and hugged him. Then pulled back and kissed him. A heart-wrenching kiss of loss and longing.

She felt his surprise, felt his arms wrap around her. She recognized the moment when he got over his surprise and kissed her back. She loved that about him.

Suddenly she was set back, cool air between them. She hated it. But she understood it. She smiled up at his hard face. "It's good to see you again."

"Damn it, Tesla." He groaned. "When do you ever stay out of trouble?"

"Ha, I was working alone when I was attacked. What was I supposed to do, ask them to come back later?"

"That's not what I meant."

She laughed. Forgetting his admonishment to be quiet until his mouth came down on hers. Hard.

She hugged him hard. In joy. She didn't want to let him go. She'd felt so alone. But he'd come for her. He set her back slightly and picked up her hands still caught in handcuffs. He studied the mechanism for a long moment then released her. He pulled out a small tool set from his back pockets and got to work.

"What about the others, are they here?"

He nodded, did something, she heard the click, and he popped the handcuff open. "Searching for you and the enemy. So far no sign of the men who attacked you."

She rubbed her wrists in relief. "Thank you. And as for the enemy…that was Daniel again. And his partner." She gave him a quick description of the second man. She could see him cataloging the details to fit into the puzzle pieces in his own mind.

"Do you know where they are?"

She shook her head. "No. Not really. When they stopped the vehicle I slipped out the back and ran. I haven't stopped since."

She sighed and ran a hand over hair. "I heard a vehicle go by but was turned around. It was a black SUV and I thought it was Daniel but wasn't sure. I figured they were heading to the highway."

"Good. It's not for you to go and look."

"I'm happy to let you chase after them and bring them down. Although I'd rather be a long way away before that happens."

"You will be. We're taking you to town. The others are going hunting."

"Town?" she asked hopefully. "As in a hot bath and a bed and would it be too much to ask for some food."

He laughed and led her out to the SUV. He knew the others were watching. He gave the signal she was unhurt and he was moving forward with the plan to retrieve the package and move her to safety. He'd be travelling with her regardless of where she went. He was on her like glue now.

It took a few hair raising hours, after making their way back to the airport they'd flown in to. But they made it.

Hours later she was flown back to her home.

Just in time for the evening's reception.

Something she had no wish to attend. But it was part of the job. If she could pull that off after the day she'd had and make it seem like nothing had gone wrong, then...

She had a shower, not as long as she'd have liked, not as hot as she'd have liked but still she was clean. There was little she could do about the damn scratches, thankfully there were none on her face. Her arms showed the mad dash through the brush still so she went for a very simple but elegant dress with long sleeves.

A quick glance in the mirror and she ginned. She'd do, although her cheek was puffy from the last hit she'd taken.

She hoped makeup had taken care of the worst of it. She

walked downstairs to find Mason in uniform whites.

She stopped, her heart beating like mad. "Don't you look wonderful," she said warmly.

He grinned. "I think I'm supposed to say that to you."

"Yes, you are," she said pertly. "So?"

He laughed. "In truth, you're glorious."

On that note, he helped her into the private car that was at her disposal and with an armed guard riding escort front and back, she was taken to the reception.

She came to a dead stop at the massive entranceway. Chandeliers glittered all around them. Women moved a short flight of steps below her, their beautiful long gowns flowing in a sea of luxury and elegance. Brilliant colors blended and shone in a glittery display of money and people in the know.

And she'd never felt so much like a fish out of water.

"Are you okay?" Mason stood at her side, a gentle hand at the small of her back.

"A few hours ago," she muttered, "I was running for my life through the brush, having escaped a horrible end. Now I'm here staring at all this glittery gold...and," her voice dropped, "wondering if I should be looking to escape all over again."

She felt his sharp glance.

"Any particular reason for wanting to bolt?"

"Someone here could have betrayed me. Many people are looking at my work with envy and might be tempted to sell me out," she answered, and when she saw his nod of agreement, she added, "And I feel like I don't belong. That I'd rather be in my sweats running the trails than trying to navigate the predators down there tonight. Not to mention, I clean up just fine but this isn't my world. I'm not comfortable in this setting with these moneyed people. I'm just me."

He slipped his arm around her lower back and tugged her slightly closer. "I'd put my money on you any day. You are more than everyone in here. You have created a program to save lives. You've done something special. You don't just clean up, you have set the standard. Now straighten up and walk down there as if you own them, because in truth – you do."

She grinned. "Thanks."

"No thanks required." He turned and waited while they were announced. "You got this."

IN FACT, SHE dominated it. Dressed in midnight navy with a hint of glitter, the fabric shimmered with every step she took. Her hair was in a deceptively simple coil on the back of her head with a long pin sticking out of one side with a matching navy jewel at the top end. She wore the same simple cross she'd had on since he'd first seen her. That was it. Classy, elegant. Money. More than that, she had presence.

He was on duty, his job to keep her safe. Not one of the guys would fault him for wanting her as his date for the evening.

She was stunning. She moved easily through the throng, deflecting questions and doing the social scene as if bred to it. And maybe she had been. Between her father and Harry, she had to have been exposed to a certain number of ceremonies. Not that they had the same social level as this big do did.

And the presentation...wow. If she was nervous she didn't show it. She spoke with calm organized thoughts, her voice easily modulating to affect the flow of information. She caught everyone's interest from her opening sentence, "I lost my brother to a land mine. I don't want to see another of our men go down from the same cause. Not when I can do something about it."

After that she had them eating out of her hands.

He was proud of her.

When she left the podium to a standing ovation, she beamed. And the world beamed back.

After that the hours passed in a mess of smiles and hand-shakes. They walked as a pair, his hand on her back or her arm hooked into his. And they felt like a pair. By the time the evening wound down, he realized they'd been holding hands for several hours.

It felt natural. Special.

Just like her.

CHAPTER 20

TESLA'S MOUTH HURT from smiling, her feet were throbbing from her killer heels and the damn scratches on her arms were driving her nuts. What had seemed like super-soft material at the beginning of the evening was now aggravating the problem with every movement. The dress needed to go and the shoes had to go now.

"Can we leave?" she asked in a low tone. She was dancing a slow waltz in his arms, loving the romance of the moment but forcing herself to remember it wasn't real. It might become real but it wasn't yet.

And he wasn't hers. Although he should be as far as her heart was concerned. Somehow he'd become very much a part of her life.

She watched as he glanced around, motioned to someone out of sight before he glanced down at her and said, "Yes, we can leave."

"Good," she whispered. "I can barely stand anymore."

"Your feet?" he asked in a harsh whisper ladened with concern.

She loved that protector part of him. "Yes, but more from the heels than the old injuries."

"The combination can't be good." He led her off the dance

floor and through the dwindling crowd.

She was so tired, she barely managed all the good-byes and thank yous as he led her outside. She waited at the doorway while the car came around, Mason standing in front of her. Then he walked her to the passenger side and helped her into the back seat. Inside she saw Swede in the front riding shotgun. She gave him a tired smile.

"I think I'd have rather had your job this evening," she said quietly. "My feet are killing me."

He grinned. "My size fourteens aren't made for high heels."

That was what she missed this last week. The teasing. The laughter. The sense of camaraderie.

"I think we might be able to find you a pair," Mason said, with a grin. "Cross-dressing has become much more popular."

Swede glared at him.

"When's your birthday?" she asked him in a teasing voice. At his horrified look, she laughed. "No worries. No high heels as gifts."

"Damn right," he muttered.

They pulled up to her house, and Swede hopped out and opened the door for her. Mason got out and came around to offer her a hand out.

"Thank you," she said to Swede and let Mason lead her into the house. She needed sleep. Tomorrow was big. As in national security big. But she had to get through tonight. She knew it was going to be a long one. She was physically and emotionally exhausted but too keyed up mentally to sleep. And she wanted to run through her program again.

There were a few things that had been bugging her in the back of her mind. She couldn't take the chance of there being a problem at this late hour.

"Bed," he said and walked her up the stairs to her room, searched the closet and bathroom then dropped to the floor to check under the bed.

He turned back to face her. "It's all clear."

She kicked off her high heels and stood for a moment in joy as her feet sank into the plush carpet. Her arches were trying to adapt to the change in position.

"So damn good," she moaned.

He laughed. "If it's so bad why do women wear them?"

"'Cause they make our legs look miles long," she said saucily. "And men love the look."

He walked closer and tugged her into his arms. "I can't argue that. You knocked them dead tonight."

She chuckled. "You mean *I'm* dead tonight."

"After the day you've had, that you managed to go at all and then ended up doing so well is fantastic. Now you need sleep."

"Are you staying here," she asked, desperately trying to keep her voice neutral.

"I am. The door will stay open and I will be on guard outside."

She nodded. Of course he was. He was on duty. She was in danger and they had to keep her safe. Feeling let down but knowing she needed to sleep alone, for everyone's sake, she turned and tilted her head forward. "Please undo the zipper. I'm not up to any fancy contortions tonight."

He slid the clasp down then stepped back. "I'll be outside if you need me."

And he walked out.

Resigned to being alone again, she watched him retreat until he was out of sight. Turning back to her closet, she slipped off her dress, hung it up then stripped down to her skin and grabbed her boy shorts tank top pajamas. It took a moment longer to take off her makeup, her arm feeling heavy and unwieldy as she finished. So damn tired.

Crossing to her bed, she pulled back the covers and crawled in. Sleep hit at the same time her head hit the pillow. She could feel her body sinking deep into the bedding. And she was out.

She woke up several hours later and rolled over. Her body ached with each shift. Why? She opened her eyes, remembering the hours of being tied up in the SUV and the panicked run through the woods. She was so damn grateful to be safe and home again. Well, maybe not home but here in a soft bed knowing she had people looking out for her. She just needed to get through tomorrow. She checked her phone. It was three in the morning.

And she hadn't gone over those few lines of code that were bugging her.

She slipped out of bed then realized her work was downstairs. She grabbed her silk robe and tied it around her waist as she walked to the door.

"Where do you think you're going?" Mason asked from the shadows.

"Earlier, something bugged me in the program. I can't sleep worrying that it might be more than a small error and need to check it out."

"You can't leave it until morning?" he asked, his voice gritty from lack of sleep. She studied him.

"How are you supposed to look after me if you're not rested?"

"I'm rested. Just waking up again. I relieved Hawk. He's sleeping downstairs. If we go down he won't get any rest."

She hesitated then shook her head. "I'll be quiet but I need to check this over."

He nodded and fell into step beside her.

Hawk was crashed on the couch, but she detoured into her office. "If it's nothing, I won't need but a moment." She hooked up a keyboard to the set of monitors.

"They took your laptop, didn't they? We never did recover it."

"Yeah, but I don't need it."

She pulled out her hard drive and booted up.

The screen lit up as they watched. She logged onto the one database she needed to check and scanned through the lines of code. Not seeing what she was looking for, she did a search. Empty. Feeling better, she went to the log to see the activity over night. Nothing.

She sighed happily.

"It's all good?" Mason asked.

"It's all good. I just need to look at one more place…"

She brought up the security files and gasped. "Except someone is trying to hack into the program."

"What? When?"

"Right now and has been for the last forty minutes." She refreshed the log. "But he stopped once I logged in."

"That makes no sense. If he's trying to log in he wouldn't know if you are logged in." He pulled up a chair and sat down beside her. "Right?"

She clicked a few keys, her mind storming through the possibilities. "Unless…"

"Unless what?"

"Did anyone contact Robert and Jordan," she asked. "I've sent them a message to let them know I'm okay. But has anyone checked in to make sure they are as well."

"I don't know." He had his phone out. "I can find out. I believe they were both contacted last night."

"Yeah, but has anything changed now, is the question."

"Why?"

"Because it looks like my employee Robert is online and can see that I'm online, that might account for the constant logging in and failing on my server and would account for them stopping as soon as they saw me online."

"But why would he stop then?"

"Because he's trying to use my log in to get on."

"And it's not working?"

"No," she said absentmindedly. "I changed it all yesterday morning before I was kidnapped."

He froze. "You changed it? Why?"

"I do as a matter of course change it every night, but yesterday morning I just wanted the extra precaution. The program was in theory done and no one needed to be working on it at all. So I locked everyone out then and moved it."

"And could they see that you'd moved it."

She frowned. "Yes, but I doubt this is a problem."

"Why, because you've worked with these people for months?"

"Years actually. Robert came on when I started this program. He was instrumental at helping me solve some bigger issues at the beginning."

"Is Robert getting paid for this?"

"Of course he is." She turned to him, her glare narrowing on his suspicious face. "What are you getting at?"

"You're set to make a substantial amount of money on this deal if it goes through, correct?"

"Yes." she nodded. "I am. So are they. I pay out bonuses and I give a lot away to charity. I always do. But we keep a year's worth of salaries in reserve to make sure we know we all have jobs."

"But this is the biggest contract ever, so in theory way more money in reserve and potentially more could have been paid out in bonuses?"

"Meaning that they are feeling hard done by. And want more?"

"Everyone wants more." He studied her face. "And what's the chance that you could have sold it for a lot more but chose not too. Which in theory means he could feel cheated."

She sat back. "It's possible. I'm not sure. There are a lot of people depending on me for their jobs. I hadn't considered that they might be looking at me as a bigger payout. Because I'm not," she admitted. "In leaner times, I took only my utilities and rent so I knew they had their wages."

"And I'm sure they appreciated that but consider that you're set to become a very wealthy woman now, and they may want a bigger slice of the pie."

She rubbed her forehead. "It's always possible. Robert wanted me to sell the program a year ago. He wasn't impressed when I refused."

"Why did you refuse?"

She drew circles aimlessly on the table top. "I wasn't going to sell it to the enemy."

Silence.

"AND HE WAS okay too?" Mason immediately texted the others. This guy needed to be picked up and questioned.

"What's happening with the program now?" he asked. "Is someone still trying to get in?"

"No. They are going to wait until I get out."

"Can they track you?" he asked in alarm.

She was busy clicking on the keyboard. "They likely are. That doesn't mean they will succeed."

He shook his head. "Damn scary, you know that."

"Yeah, but not the first time this has happened. Still, given the timing definitely suspicious."

"When did it happen last time?"

"About a year ago."

She leaned closer, her focus on the screen in front of her. None of what she was doing made any sense to him. There was nothing legible on the screen but it was scrolling at a fast pace, so he knew she couldn't be reading it, yet she gave every impression of doing so.

She hit the last key extra hard and a window opened. A small one with a white box in the middle and a series of numbers and periods. She highlighted it and opened yet another window.

Mason wanted to know what she was doing but didn't want to disturb her.

At the new screen, she popped in the number he belatedly realized was an IP address and realized she was tracking the person trying to break into her system.

"Do you have someone close to Robert's place?" she asked

quietly. "If so, have someone go in and make sure he's alive."

"Why?"

"This is coming from his place. But it's very much not his style of writing."

"How can you tell?" he asked, staring at the screen. "There is no writing anywhere to be found."

"He writes code but not splashed on the page full of garbage. His code is very clean and elegant. Something he takes pride in."

"Where does he live?" Mason asked.

"Several hours away," Hawk said, yawning at the doorway. "We need to have someone else there faster than that."

Mason grabbed up his phone. "We'll find someone."

CHAPTER 21

NOW THAT SHE had done what she'd planned to do, and the worry shifted to something from her mind to action, she felt worn out and back to being tired again. She checked her program, doubled up on the security with a few clicks and locked it down. She had it on her hard drive as well, but no one would know and they wouldn't be able to get into it on there either.

"Tired?"

"Yeah." She stopped mid yawn, and gave a small laugh. "Sorry, I guess I'm more tired than I thought."

"Come on, you can lie down while we handle this."

She nodded. "If you're sure there's nothing I can do, I should try to grab some more sleep."

He walked her back up to her bedroom. She crawled into bed, pulling the covers up over her shoulder.

"Good night."

Silently, he walked out to the hallway to stand guard.

She loved it. And she hated it. She wanted him here with her.

"Mason?"

He came running. She smiled. "I don't suppose you could lie down beside me. Make it easier to sleep."

He immediately lay down on the bed and rolled over to face

her. "Sleep," he whispered. "It's all good. Just close your eyes and drop off to sleep."

She closed her eyes obediently. Then the wonderful cologne he wore teased her nose. She'd been drifting through it all night at the reception. She didn't think she'd ever be able to smell it without thinking of him. And he was something.

"You're not sleeping."

"I can't. You smell too good." She opened her eyes and grinned at his startled expression. "You smell wonderful. Male. Strong. Caring."

"Hey, those are hardly scents. They are all qualities. And hardly fit me."

She leaned up on her elbow and stared down at him. "They are so much like you," she teased. "Look at you."

He chuckled. "You're sweet and delusional."

She snickered. "So not." She shoved her face toward him. "Kiss me."

His eyebrows shot up. He leaned closer, and with his lips a hairbreadth from hers, whispered, "Why would I?"

"Because I want to feel your lips on mine."

Heat flashed.

Under hooded gaze he whispered so close to her that his warm breath wafted over her lips, "It's not a good idea."

"I think it's a wonderful idea." She couldn't resist pushing the line. It wasn't fair. It wasn't right. But she desperately wanted him.

"It's a terrible idea. You need your sleep."

"I need you." Her lips brushed against his once, then twice. In a teasing manner she pulled back slightly so she could look in his eyes and saw the hesitation in them. Too damn honorable for his own good. She dropped her elbow down and rolled onto her back, hooking her arms around his neck, tugging him down on top of her.

"It's still not – mphff."

She sealed his lips with the kiss she'd been wanting to give him since she saw him standing downstairs waiting for her this evening. He was gorgeous. He wasn't hers but maybe for a night…or even a few hours…he could be.

Then she didn't have to hold him close at all. Because he was holding her against his heart, kissing her as she'd always wanted to be kissed by him and couldn't. He was sleek, hot and there was such a sense of freedom.

She snuggled up close. Tonight was special. A moment of time stolen. Stealing had never been her thing, but right now, she'd take everything she could get if it was him. He was everything she wanted and knew she'd never be able to handle. Harry had been such a big figure in her life that all other men had paled beside him. Until she met Mason.

"Are you sure?" He dropped a kiss on her nose, her cheek, her chin.

"I'm sure." She tugged his head down and kissed him hard, trying to let him know how much she wanted this. Wanted him. Surely he'd understand without the words.

But still he hesitated. She sighed, her warm breath bathing them both in steamy heat. "What's bothering you?"

He pulled back slightly and looked down at her. She smiled. "I'm on the pill if that's what's the matter."

His gaze lit and he smiled. "I'm glad to hear that."

She smiled and looped her arms around his neck. "Then love me, Mason. For tonight. For right now." She breathed in his scent, nuzzling the side of his neck. "Please."

And that last word seemed to break his stiffness. His sense of honor. Something here was bothering him, and if she could think, she'd likely come up with what it was. Only she didn't want to think, she just wanted to feel.

To be with him for this moment in time.

She reached down and tugged his shirt tail out of his pants, searching for the skin below. Frantic at first, then stilling when she made contact, her fingers stroked and kneaded his heavy muscle ridge down his spine. So muscled, so hard. So damn...male.

She loved it.

He shifted back and kneeled in front of her, his fingers quickly undoing the buttons on his shirt and ripping it off his shoulders. She sat up and reached for the heavily muscled chest. She ran her fingers over the rippled abs and up to the pectoral muscles bulging as he shrugged out of his shirt. Leaning over, she flicked his nipples with her tongue, then scraped her teeth across the sensitive skin. He moaned. She smiled and bit gently, her nails scraping up over his stomach before stroking down over his shoulders and arms.

"So damn perfect."

"Yes, you are." He hopped off the bed, stripped off his pants while she watched. When she reached for him, he slid back onto the bed and clasped her head on either side to hold her still for his deep tongued kiss. She melted against him, loving the way his erection prodded her belly. She cuddled closer, her hips instinctively hugging his erection. There was nothing like the feeling of being close to him. Of knowing she was his woman for tonight. Not crying about tomorrow. Not knowing what tomorrow would bring. She'd take what she could and deal with the rest later.

His hands slid down to rest on her collarbone and lower still to cup her plump breasts. They rested there for a long moment then slid down her ribs and around her back to her buttocks. His fingers dug in, and he pulled her hard against his erection. She wiggled closer yet again, striving to rise high so the fit would be perfect. He flipped her down to lie on the bed where he paused and just looked his fill. "So beautiful," he whispered.

She smiled and arched her back toward him. "I'm glad you think so."

He stroked his hands up the side of her thighs and hips and across her belly. While she rolled her hips in his direction, he slipped a finger behind the edge of her boy panties. She gasped, her pelvis rising in response. It had been such a long time. He smoothed his fingers across the front of her panties, adding slight pressure over her mound. She swallowed, her gaze locked on the fascination of his face. As if he was really loving this.

She shifted her legs wide, making a place for him. He smiled and stroked a finger down her crotch and over the wet spot. He slid a finger along the elastic of the legs just inside, enough to tantalize and not enough to satisfy. She shivered.

He teased her a little more, then in one movement, swooped her panties and tossed them off to the side. Now she lay open to his view. He lowered his head and kissed her belly button. She reached to tug him toward her. He came willingly, sliding down along her skin. Dropping tiny kisses along his path, he made his way up her belly and ribs before stopping to give each breast his attention. They both appreciated it, nipples plumping in pleasure. She tugged him all the way up to her mouth.

"Enough teasing," she whispered.

He kissed her hard. "Never."

And gently slipped inside her. And out again, then he entered a little bit more. Each time seating himself slightly deeper and deeper. She shifted and tried to relax, to give him passage, but it had been so damn long.

He paused, reached down and held her hips firm…and plunged.

She groaned.

His lips stroked across hers, giving her a moment to adjust. "You okay?"

She nodded. "It's just been awhile," she admitted.

"Good," he whispered, shifting so he was resting on his elbows. With gentle strokes he ran his finger through her hair, massaging and caressing skin. He kissed her lips lightly once, twice and then a third time.

She relaxed, her muscles easing around him, letting him go deeper and deeper. He lifted slightly and pushed in deeper until he was to the hilt.

She sighed. "Nice."

He smiled. "Sweetie, that's nothing yet."

He gathered her into his arms and drove into her again and again. Her body responded like she'd never done before. She tossed and turned and chanted his name and still he drove them both on. When she didn't think she could stand it anymore, he reached down between them and found her center. Just that gentle touch…and she was flung off the cliff as a glorious climax ripped through her.

He drove in once more, his back arching, a low groan escaping, before he collapsed down beside her.

Tears in her eyes, she cuddled close.

She'd steal this bit of time every damn chance she could get.

MASON WOKE WITH a sudden start. The hawk's cry from inside the house caught his attention. He slipped off the bed, taking care to not wake her up and dressed quickly. He was outside in the hallway within seconds. But it was already too late to keep anything private between them. He pulled out this phone to check for messages. Nothing. Good.

Hawk slipped around the corner. "Mason?"

"I'm here."

Hawk nodded. He glanced inside and saw Tesla sleeping. "Good. She needs it."

"She does. What's up?"

"Cooper checked on Robert." He stopped and pulled out his phone. "There was no sign of anyone at the house."

"So she was wrong?" Mason asked in surprise. Weird, it never occurred to him she might be.

"No, I don't think so. There were signs of a struggle, and he left without his vehicle and there didn't appear to be anything packed up." He dropped the phone into his pocket. "Cooper is tracking the money right now. He'll get back to me as soon as he finds something."

"Right. That could give us some answers."

Hawk nudged him toward the room. "It's my watch. Go back and lie down. You need sleep too. And..." He cast a long narrow gaze at Tesla in the bed. "She's not sleeping well without you."

Mason twisted enough to look at the bed. True enough, Tesla was whimpering in her sleep.

"Damn. It took forever for her to sleep. She's plagued by nightmares."

"I don't blame her. She's been kidnapped twice." Hawk sighed. "We all get nightmares. We have a good reason. Now so does she."

Mason winced. "True enough."

"Go."

After a quick glance toward Hawk and reassured that his friend had his back, Mason went and lay down. Instantly Tesla curled up against him. He wrapped an arm around her and tugged her closer.

And fell asleep.

For bare moments. His phone went off. He read the orders and frowned. He glanced down at Tesla. He hated to leave her. But there was a problem that needed attention. Someone had been seen entering the Hall. Had to be checked out. He sent a quick message back asking if someone else could do the check as he was on duty.

The response was immediate. She was asleep and had guards inside and out. He needed to do this and fast.

Damn it. He stared suspiciously at the orders. There was nothing untoward about them. Just he hated to leave her alone. And this was pulling him away.

Still, it was something that had to be checked.

Nothing could go wrong this day. He couldn't argue that. With a last glance at Tesla, he slipped downstairs. He found Hawk in the living room and filled him in on the orders.

Hawk shrugged at his buddy's frown. "It is what it is."

With a last look upstairs, he said, "Take good care of her."

And he walked out into the night.

CHAPTER 22

S HE WOKE TO the birds singing and the sun shining. It was a glorious day. Then she remembered what today was. And what last night had been. She bolted upright. The other side of the bed was empty. The room was empty. She was nude. And her body hummed in joy. Satiated from the best loving in her life, she threw back her covers and bounded off the mattress. A check of her cell phone said it was early yet.

Good. A shower was first, followed by putting on her jeans and sweater until it was time to get ready. It was early and she didn't want to spend more time in her suit and pumps than she had to. Afterwards, she twirled in front of the mirror, happy with her life. She twisted her hair back and up, looking to keep it from flying around her head.

Nothing could be allowed to distract her today.

She needed all her wits about her for this demonstration.

Mason would be with her all day, but she had no idea in what role. And after today, she was likely to never see him again.

Her heart jerked at the thought but knew it was inevitable. She'd known they weren't to be since the beginning. She held her head up and shoved that thought to the back of her mind. Her priorities were clear.

She straightened her clothing once again. Lord she was nervous. After several deep bracing breaths she walked to the kitchen.

Coffee was set up. She clicked the power button to set it dripping. Where was Mason? Swede? Hawk? Surely she wasn't alone? Then she realized maybe it was all good now. Relieved but still wary, she pulled out a mug and thieved a cup of coffee. Then walked to her office. Standing at the entrance she studied the small room. It appeared to be as she'd left it. Good.

Her nerves were rubbing her wrong. There was so much hanging on this deal.

It wasn't even the money. It was all about saving lives.

For Harry.

She turned to look around. As far as she could tell, she was alone. She frowned. She shouldn't be, should she? She walked out to the back yard and wandered the small green patch aimlessly. There was no gardener today, and no one else that she could see within reach. How did that work? She wandered back inside, feeling her nerves tighten in worry.

Pulling out her cell phone, she checked the time. She still had hours to go. Determined to stay busy, she sat down at her computer and logged on. Her emails were first.

She ran though the ones she'd been expecting.

And came to one she hadn't.

The subject said, "Robert's life."

Frowning, she clicked on it. And froze. She snatched up her phone and called Robert. No answer. She redialed and again, no answer. She left a voice message and logged onto the company account. He wasn't online. She checked with another employee. She was online. She sent her an instant message asking if she'd had any contact with Robert.

The answer came back immediately. *No. Not since noon yes-*

terday.

Tesla brought out phone again. And called Mason.

"Tesla, what's up?"

He sounded like he was driving from the noises of a radio coming through him.

"Where are you?" she asked, her voice tremulous.

"I'm almost at the house. Why?"

"There's something you need to see."

"Be there in a few minutes. Have you shown Hawk?"

She took a raspy gasp. "He's not here. I'm alone."

There was a moment of shocked silence. "Get up and move very quietly to the bathroom where I want you to lock yourself in."

She stood up and looked around. She locked the back door and then the front. And ran up the stairs. "I'm going upstairs," she whispered, her heart pounding against her chest. "Where's Hawk?"

"I don't know," he said. "I was called away over a security problem at the main hall where you're to do your demonstration."

The bathroom was in sight. She raced inside and slammed the door shut. And locked it. Taking a deep breath, her hand trembling, she turned, intent on checking that the shower was empty.

And was snatched from behind.

She gave a strangled scream but a blow came out of nowhere and caught the side of her head and cut off the sound as she slumped to the floor. She couldn't speak or hear for the ringing in her head.

Still numb but aware, unable to move, she was dragged to

the living room. And tossed onto the floor.

Another man grabbed her and picked her up, slamming her to the chair. Seconds later she was tied and helpless. She tried to hold back the panic, but when the first blow hit her across her face, a whimper escaped.

"Talk."

She stayed silent. Oh God. This was her worst nightmare come true. Third time lucky for the bastards. It was now or never. This morning was everything. She either gave in and died now or didn't give in and died in a few moments. She'd go the second route, and give Mason's men those few extra minutes he and the team needed to get to her. At least he knew she was in trouble. As calmly as she could manage, she asked, "Where's Hawk?"

A different man laughed behind her. She closed her eyes, recognizing the voice. Daniel.

Shit.

"He's...indisposed."

A euphemism for dead. And that would be her fate, he was warning her, if she didn't give them what they wanted.

"Now, talk."

She shook her head. "No."

The next blow sent her flying. The chair tumbled sideways and she landed on her arms, her head snapping down to the floor. The blow stunned her and she lay struggling to catch her breath.

One of the other men righted her. She moaned.

"Talk."

"No."

Another blow.

And on it went.

She lost track of time. The only thought in her mind was to endure. Survive. To be there alive for when Mason arrived. He'd come. She knew he'd come.

Into a trap.

MASON WAS ALREADY racing to the house. He had to get her out of there safely. In his heart he knew Hawk had a chance if the enemy hadn't popped him immediately. If they had, well he had another reason to kill these bastards.

He drove like a crazy man through town. The rest of the team were converging on the house. But that didn't mean she'd be there when he arrived.

He was minutes away. Minutes she didn't have. He had to make it.

His communicator beeped. "We're in position."

"ETA is two minutes. What can you see?"

"Nothing. The curtains are closed. The cottage is silent. Not a sound."

Shit. He made a hard right turn and then a left. She was just a minute away. Dear God, let him be in time.

Swede spoke. "I can see into the kitchen. All clear."

He ripped up to the correct block, pulled off and parked out of sight. "On foot. Approaching from the road. Going silent."

He put away the phone and ran forward. He could see several men on the road. He knew the others would be ready. He slipped to the front door and listened. Swede would be entering through the kitchen. The others through the windows. He checked his watch, three, two, one. He burst through the front door and raced into the small cottage.

There was no one in the living room. He spun through the house, Swede coming in through the back door. "Where is she?"

He shook his head in denial of the truth. He ran through the hall to the bedroom, his heart stopping at the sight of the bed where he'd spent the night with her. And found nothing. The bathroom. The closets.

Returning to the living room, he caught sight of Swede. And the horrible truth on his face.

She was gone. Again.

CHAPTER 23

PAIN RADIATED FROM the top of her body down. The only good thing was Hawk lay beside her, blood oozing from his skull. Not a bad head wound hopefully, but he hadn't regained consciousness yet and that worried her.

It was hard to see through her swollen eyes, but she could make out that his chest rose and fell with each breath. If he could get help, then he'd likely survive. Like Mason, he was tough. And like Mason he'd worked his way into her heart. She hurt for him. And the others. They wouldn't handle it well if they found the two of them dead.

Poor Mason.

She couldn't do that to him.

But she might not have a choice.

She didn't even remember when they stopped hitting her. She'd passed out before they ran out of fun. How long until the assholes came back. She rolled over and spat out a mouthful of blood. Gathering her strength, she pulled up onto her knees.

That was the first time she realized she wasn't tied up. She glanced around, looking for a way out. There was a door to the left. She couldn't hear anyone on the other side. But Hawk came first. She shuffled toward him. Other than his head injury, he appeared to be fine. Other than that...she almost laughed then almost cried at the pain the laugh caused. "Crap."

Well, she could talk, so that was something. If that guttural sound was talking. She smacked Hawk gently on the cheek. "Hawk, wake up."

He didn't move. She leaned down and whispered in his ear. "Hawk, I need you. Wake up, please. We're prisoners." She picked up his hand and squeezed it. When she thought she felt a faint response, she squeezed harder. "Hawk, please wake up. They are likely to come back at any minute."

The floor shifted beneath her. She froze. Earthquake? No not possible. She waited for it to happen again. And this time the shift was more of a roll. Water. They were on a boat. Shit. Now she shook Hawk. She needed him awake. She could swim, but she doubted she could keep an unconscious Hawk afloat. She wasn't that strong a swimmer.

She couldn't leave him alone. "Hawk," she snapped, trying to interject some military harshness to her voice. It's what he was used to after all. "Wake up," she ordered.

She waited and watched. And was rewarded with a slight movement of his eyelids. Excited, she bent down and talked to him again. Explaining where they were and what had happened. "You have to wake up, please."

He moaned slightly and slowly opened his eyes. There was an unfocused look to his gaze. "Hawk, it's Tesla. Wake up and stay quiet."

His gaze sharpened and then suddenly they came into focus. She smiled encouragingly at him. "That's better. You need to be careful when you move. You were hit on the head and are still bleeding. You've been out for a long time."

His gaze roamed her face.

"They are likely to come back any time. That's the only thing," she said apologetically. "And I'm afraid we might be on a boat."

His gaze sharpened. "Your face," he said in cold and clear tones. "What happened to your face?"

She reached up and gently touched her hot face. "They hit me because I wouldn't tell them anything." She dropped her head and whispered, "I'm not sure what they'll do when they come back."

"You won't be here," he promised.

"Maybe and maybe not," she said, hoping he was going to be well enough to leave, but not so sure at this point. She studied his white face in concern. "You *are* injured."

He sat up slowly and quickly checked his body over. When he reached his head, he winced. "Could use a shot of whiskey right now but other than a headache, I'm fine." He climbed to his feet and helped her up. She gasped as she straightened.

"Ribs?"

"I don't know," she whispered. "Maybe."

He ran his hands over her in a professional manner and nodded. "Looks like they've cracked a couple. Those bastards," he said between clenched teeth.

"Daniel and two others," she whispered, wishing he hadn't said cracked and ribs in the same sentence. Now they hurt, damn it.

"They will pay."

She nodded, not worrying about that right now. "We need to get back. I don't have much time before my demonstration."

She felt more than saw his startled gaze. She stared at the door. "Do we just open it? See what's out there?" She hated the fear in her voice. Hated the fear in her soul.

"Did you tell them anything?" Hawk asked. "Thought I heard some of the questioning but can't be sure what I was hearing."

"No, I didn't," she whispered, wrapping her arms around her chest. "But I wanted to." She raised a shamed glance to meet his bravely. "I'm sorry."

He gave her a gentle smile. "For what? For being human?"

"It's so easy to fail," she admitted.

"But you didn't. Now," he grabbed her arm slightly and nudged her toward the door. "I'll sneak out first."

She nodded. She hated to see his shaky steps as he made his way to the door, but as if every step gave him strength, by the time he was at the door he stood tall. Ready. She straightened, gaining strength from him. Thank God she wasn't alone.

"MASON. WE HAVE received notice that a yacht was taken out on the lake this morning."

Mason turned to look at Swede. "A yacht?"

"Not a big luxury schooner we might associate with the name, but a small tight ship that had been rented for a week. They brought it back last night and handed it over. But then this morning it was gone from its mooring."

"The same people?" he asked, frowning. Wondering why they'd have taken a boat out. Unless it was because no one could hear her scream. The thought made his stomach heave. The lake was huge. And the weather rough and wild and erratic. He had no idea if this missing boat had anything to do with Tesla or not, but they had little to go on. However, it was a short hop over the back wall to the neighboring town and down to the dock. He slowly stiffened and walked back outside. Swede at his side. They both studied the back wall.

"It would be easy," Swede said. "Carry her over the wall and to the neighbors."

"Who happen to be gone for a week." Mason frowned. "But why take Hawk?"

"To leave nothing behind."

Mason nodded. There could be other reasons, but that made the most sense. If he had the manpower. And if Hawk wasn't dead. "He's still alive. He has to be. Otherwise they'd have left him in place."

"I have a better idea why they took Hawk."

Mason turned to look at Shadow. His smile was harshly thin. "To force Tesla to give them what they want." He paused. "She's proven a little too stubborn for their liking at this point and having someone else to beat up would make her more cooperative."

"Ha," Mason snapped. "Not even that will help."

"But they don't know that," Shadow said with the merest of a smile.

A call came from the hall. It was Dane. "The two men stationed outside have been found. Dead."

"That's how they got inside then. And likely out. Okay. Tear the two houses apart looking for answers."

"Not sure we need to. The owner of the second house owns a boat. The same one that went missing off the marina this morning."

"And the owner?"

"We're trying to contact him. He's somewhere in Ireland on

a hike I understand. So far, no luck in finding just where."

"Find him. And we're after the boat." He looked over at Swede. "Let's go."

CHAPTER 24

TESLA WAITED FOR Hawk to peer out the door. She worried about his head. He looked dangerous as hell and as mean as a rattlesnake. She loved it. He shoved her behind him. He was awfully arrogant though. Although Mason was worse. Hawk opened the door wider and stepped out. She caught her breath. If she could see easier she wouldn't be so panicked. Actually, yeah she would.

He held out a hand. She grabbed it and slipped out into the tiny hallway. The boat was listing to the side now. He raced along the hallway to the small door up ahead. He tried to open it, but it wouldn't budge. It was locked. She groaned, but he did something she couldn't see and the door popped open.

With care, he opened it wide enough for her to see a set of stairs in front of them. And something else.

She grabbed his hand and squeezed, then pointed to the floor.

Water was seeping in.

He nodded. Leading her up the four stairs he lifted his head to the boat deck and peered around.

"Is anyone there?" she whispered.

He held his hand up to stop her from talking then motioned for her to stay there. She nodded. Where the hell could she go?

She looked around. They were on a boat somewhere out in the middle of nowhere. She spun around, just her head visible but could see nothing geographical around them but water. Including rising up her feet.

He raced back to her. "Come on. It's empty and sinking fast."

She swallowed hard. "They were going to kill us this time, weren't they?"

He nodded. "If you hadn't woken me when you did, I'd be gone already."

She looked back and realized the water was up the second stair. They had minutes only. "Is there a dinghy, a rowboat, something to help?"

"No." In a sudden movement, he asked, "Can you swim?"

"Yes," she said hesitantly. "But not that well." She stared out at the water and the foggy conditions. They were miles from land. "Do we stay with the boat?"

"For as long as she's above water, but we need to find something that floats to help support us."

"Right."

But she hadn't even digested his comment before he was stripping off the large cushions from the driver and passenger seats. Straps he cut from somewhere had the two floats tied together. She felt better when she saw that. The last thing she wanted was to get separated from him.

"Are they watching us?"

"Not likely. They've gone." He stopped what he was doing. "Did they get it?"

She stared at him. Her hand went to the cross on her necklace and gripped it tight. "They might have taken the hard drive and the rest of my computer equipment, but they didn't get the program."

He grinned. "Excellent."

"But they could have whatever Robert had at his place."

Hawk froze. "And what did he have?"

"Parts of it," she admitted. "Early prototype."

"Is it enough?"

"No."

"Good enough."

"Do we know what happened to him?"

"Not yet."

HAWK REFRAINED FROM telling her that there was no way the kidnappers would let Robert live. If he'd betrayed her, he was dead because they couldn't trust him. If he hadn't betrayed her, he was dead because he wouldn't give them what they wanted. And if he hadn't given it over right away then he'd be so badly injured, he'd be dead anyway.

She was smart enough to figure it out on her own.

He knew the team would be here soon. They'd have tracked them down by now. What she hadn't figured out was that with cracked ribs, swimming was going to be a bitch. He needed to get her to safety fast. Under the back seat he found a set of oars. He grinned. Now they were talking.

There were minutes left before the boat sunk fully. Precious minutes he needed.

Then the time was gone and they were in the water. Tesla on the float and holding on, fear on her face. He wasn't afraid of the water. This was his domain. His preferred medium for any warfare. They wanted to come. Let them. He'd give them a surprise.

As if his thoughts had conjured them up, he heard sounds of a boat motoring toward them. He could hope it was a rescue, but...

A piece of pipe was strung through his belt loop, his ankle knife was in his hand, and he slipped into the cold water.

Frigid water. And he realized they had a bigger enemy now. The temperature was deadly. They had maybe forty minutes before she'd be numb. He yelled at her. "Climb on fully. The temperature is too cold for us to last very long."

She gazed at him in surprise then understanding. With effort she climbed, and he could see the moment the ribs screamed as she pulled herself on top. Then she reached out a hand to help him.

He stared at it.

He was a SEAL, this was his domain, and she, injured and hurting, was trying to help him get out of the cold water.

She was something.

CHAPTER 25

"**H**ELP!" SHE CRIED out to the approaching vessel. "Help."
No response.

Shit. It was a power boat. Large with someone dressed in black. And she knew this rescue wasn't going to go well. Damn it. She shifted higher so Hawk was hidden from sight.

"Help!"

Still no response. There wasn't much left of the boat they originally woke up on. In fact, just a few bits of loose debris floated beside her. She grabbed a water bottle that floated by. She'd take that.

The boat came alongside. The man in black walked to the side closest to her. And held out a hand.

She didn't recognize him.

But she had limited choices. She reached up and caught his hand. He gave a rough tug and pulled her aboard. She groaned as her ribs took more abuse. Then he helped her to sit down. So maybe a rescuer? But she didn't believe in fairy tales anymore.

"Thank you," she said, her breath coming out in short gasps. The slide over the side of the boat hadn't done anything good for her ribs. She closed her eyes for a long moment, trying to regain her balance.

When she opened her swollen eyes it was to find him standing in front of her. A short snub looking handgun pointing at her.

"It's just not my day, is it?" she muttered, glaring at him. "Who the hell are you?"

"You're luckier than you know," he snapped. "I work with Daniel. And the assholes who kidnapped you weren't supposed to leave you on the ship to die. But that's all right, the asshole that did is paying for his error right now."

"I don't know anything," she whispered, wondering if she could make it over the railing. She'd rather take her chance with the water than be back in the hands of these assholes. "Or I'd have told them."

"No, you wouldn't. You're too damn noble. And for what?"

She straightened. If she had to do this one more time, then well, she would. Inside she was afraid. What if she couldn't hold out again? What if she gave in? No. She couldn't give in.

And yet…she eyed the gun.

"Are you the one paying them to do this to me? Where's Daniel?"

"Daniel got called away. The presentation you did last night caused the buyers some angst. Daniel is trying to keep things on an even keel. Now the men downstairs? One is punishing the other for sinking the boat with you. You weren't supposed to die."

"Why did you kill the other man with me?" she whispered, pretending Hawk was dead. "He didn't do anything to you."

"Maybe not, but he would have." The man shrugged. "He's a SEAL. He wouldn't be able to help himself."

"Damn it." She reached up and rubbed her eyes. Everything hurt. The world was in a dismal state if people like this had nothing better to do but screw around with others and hurt people for fun.

"The money for you is better than most contracts." He snorted. "But you are only valuable if your damn software comes with it."

Ah. So that was what was wrong. "And he figured that as I didn't have it that I was useless and best to let me die."

"Exactly. Then again, getting good help these days is a bitch." He smiled. "But it all worked out in the end."

She nodded as if she understood when in truth she didn't understand anything.

"Now that we have you again, we'll toss you to the buyer. Along with the electronics we recovered from your employee."

"Is Robert dead?" She glared at him. She might just kill him herself if he was.

"Nah, not yet. But he's going to wish he was. He promised the goods and he didn't deliver."

She closed her eyes. Damn it. Maybe Mason had been right. Had Robert been after a bigger payday?

"This has been a shitty job from start to finish." The gunman growled, "What's with you damn people."

"So finish it now," she snapped.

The gun spun around and faced her again.

"I'd be happy to, but I want my fucking paycheck."

Her chest seized. She gasped for breath, struggling to get the air locked inside back out. But it wasn't happening. She made a harsh wheezing sound and watched as the boat swam before her panicked eyes.

"Fuck." A harsh pound on her back had the old air gushing out and new air rushing in. She collapsed to the deck in pain…but alive.

"Enough of that shit."

He turned around again and walked up to the pilot house. And fired up the engines again. She briefly wondered about throwing herself over the side of the boat again, but the floatation seat cushions were nowhere in sight. And neither was Hawk.

HAWK CROUCHED BEHIND the cabin, dripping water over the side of the boat. He watched as Tesla collapsed to the ground wheezing, but at least she was breathing again. He'd only seen the one man. There had to be more.

He slipped down the stairs and into the stateroom. At the bedroom he studied the room through the small panes of glass. Two men, one dead or dying and one stretched out on the bed, his arms crossed under his head. His damn phone resting on his chest.

The sleeping man appeared to be the guy who had taken Tesla to the airstrip with Daniel. He gave a brief look to the other man but didn't recognize him. Someone who screwed up and was paying for it. He gripped the piece of pipe in his hand and went in high and strong and aiming for the asshole's knees. This guy wasn't going to walk away again.

Instinct had the man waking just at Hawk's pipe came down – to the bed – the empty space where the man's legs had been.

Hawk launched himself at the bed, adjusting his position at the last minute, and plowed his fist into the asshole's face. Then a quick slam of his pipe. Damn, it was off target. The other man roared and tackled him to the ground. Jammed between the bed and the built in cabinets, the fight was fast and fierce.

But Hawk had the upper hand.

And he was fighting for Tesla.

Hawk was broadside a few moments later. And the second fight was on, this time with the man who'd brought Tesla onboard. Only Hawk found himself flat on his back before he knew what had happened and the asshole had his big thick hands wrapped around his neck. Hawk gasped and struggled to flip him over his back when suddenly he was free and the enemy was fighting for his own life. Tesla had launched herself on the behemoth's back, and with some kind of strap she'd wrapped the man's neck and twisted tight, strangling him.

The man jerked back, trying to free himself, but Hawk tripped him up and knocked him down. Tesla went flying and Hawk brought the pipe down on the man's head. And again.

He didn't move again.

Crying and laughing, Tesla launched herself at him. "Oh my God, you're alive. I was so worried."

Hawk was damn near insulted. "I'm fine," he said. "Are you?"

"I'm great." She laughed, then gasped, her hand going to her side. "Okay, so maybe not so great." She pointed toward the stairs. "I think there are other men below."

"No," Hawk said in a hard voice. "There *were* men below."

"Oh." In a small voice she asked, "Did you kill them?"

What did she think he'd do? Sit them down and spank them? Well, he had in a way, he'd spanked the one with a metal pipe.

"No, the one man had already done a good job of trying to kill the other." He spun around searching the fog. "We need to get to shore."

She nodded. "Do you have a way to communicate with the others?"

He nodded. "The ship's radio if nothing else."

With that he hopped up to the wheelhouse, and playing with a few knobs, clicked a display. Crackling noises filled the air. With her watching his every movement, he soon had the radio working. He sent a message to Mason first. Then he checked the gas and started up the engine that had been previously shut down. He motored slowly to the wreckage of the other boat and marked the GPS location for someone to clean it up and so the authorities would know there'd been no loss of life in the accident.

Then he turned the vessel, and its dead cargo, toward shore.

Tesla settled into the passenger seat beside him, curling up against the bitter wind. It would be a nice day at this hour, but on the lake in the fog there was nothing but a deep chilliness that seemed to seep into the bones.

"You saved my life," she whispered from somewhere around her knees. He couldn't see her face, just the top of her head as it burrowed deeper against her legs. He looked around but couldn't see a blanket. And he had no intention of sending her below. Not with the men down there. He knew the one was gone and doubted the other was still alive. He'd get medical attention as soon as they could get it but suspected it would still be a good twenty minutes.

It wasn't likely that he had that long.

"Do you think this is done?"

There was no misunderstanding her meaning after all the shit they'd been through. "It damn well better be," he said, leaning across to rub her shoulder. "Regardless, we've got your back."

She smiled mistily up at him, and as she lay her head back down on her knees, she whispered, "Thank you."

He shook his head. "You saved my life and you're thanking me." Who knew there were women out there like her? She was Mason's. No doubt there. But she was damn fine. If Mason didn't want her, Hawk wouldn't mind a chance.

She was some kind of woman. He took another look over at her and realized she'd curled up like a kitten and slept.

Yeah, she was some kind of woman.

He steered the boat to shore. With any luck she'd get enough sleep to be able to handle what was coming.

CHAPTER 26

W HEN SHE WOKE, the wind was biting and swirling through the small cabin. The sun was trying to shine, but it was held back by the fog. And although lifting, the fog didn't appear ready to give up its domain.

Tesla had hoped Mason would be here by now. Wherever here was. She just wanted to get the hell home. And even that couldn't happen. She had to go to the damn demonstration. Looking the way she did. Great.

She could probably push it off for a few days, but then this hell would continue. Better to suffer through the demonstration and then go hide away and lick her wounds. If Mason found her then, that was a whole different story.

Right now, they all had a job to do.

She was just so damn tired of doing it.

Through the fog, she could see a shoreline take shape. She smiled. Now that was a mighty fine picture. She stood up to see better. "Any idea where we are?"

"I'm not sure." But from the dark tone to his voice, she thought he might but didn't want to tell her.

He grabbed the radio. "Penderson Marina. That's the name I can see."

He clicked off and waited for a response. When it came she

didn't quite understand. Until Hawk said, "Okay, we're going to be about an hour then unless you can arrange a ride to pick us up."

He nodded at the next response and shut down the radio. "We have car and a helicopter on the way."

At the word helicopter her heart sank. Then she realized after all she'd been through, how damn appropriate this would be. She'd arrive in style and to hell with them all. She'd come to do a job for those men. She'd do it and go home.

She sat in silence as Hawk handled the boat with enviable skill. She had no idea how long he'd been doing this, but he made it all look easy.

The weather was clear by the time he pulled up to a mooring spot and hopped off, tying the boat up securely. He glanced around and saw what he was looking for. He motioned to the dock. She gasped at the sea of uniforms racing toward them.

Hawk helped her out of the boat and stood with her as the men came and ushered her to a waiting car. She was driven to a small helicopter pad and loaded up and within minutes she was airborne.

Hawk still at her side.

She glanced down and realized she was no longer scared. She'd been through so much shit already, riding in a helicopter was no biggie.

"You're not worried this time?"

She grinned. "Nah, why would I be? Mason's not here."

He frowned, his gaze searching. "What difference would that make?"

"Tons," she said with a laugh. "He's not here to throw me out."

Hawk laughed and laughed. "Wait until I tell him that."

"If he doesn't like the answer, he should have been here," she cried. "Would that have been so hard?"

"You know he's going to blame himself for this, right?"

She twisted in her seat. "Why would he?"

"He had to leave to make sure the security was in place for the day. When he left, the enemy moved in."

She nodded slowly. "I knew but hadn't considered how long he'd be gone. Figured he'd gotten busy."

"He'd never have left without it being a direct order."

"He was ordered to leave?" At Hawk's nod, she smiled. "That makes me feel better, but maybe someone should be asking the hard questions as to who ordered him away."

Hawk sat back and stared at her. "You think military are involved?"

She laughed. "Hawk, at this point, I suspect everyone but you and the rest of the team."

That beautiful white toothed grin flashed. "Glad to hear that."

They landed soon after and were quickly transferred to another car. Inside, she caught Hawk glancing at his watch.

"How close are we?"

"They started the opening speech a few minutes ago."

"Oh good, I'm glad to miss that. Hate those things."

Hawk barked with laughter and she grinned. "What do you think? Should I go like this?" She motioned to her blood stained clothing.

"It would be unique," he said.

"But it would also be the truth. And I'm all about that."

It was taking a chance, but if someone in that room had given the order to pull Mason back off the house and leave Hawk vulnerable to the enemy then maybe they should see that they failed first-hand.

"Don't give them any warning," she said suddenly. "Just tell them we'll be on time."

"Are you sure?"

She nodded. "Did you find out who ordered Mason off the protection detail?"

He shook his head. "I'm asking him that now."

"Find out before I go in, then find that man in the audience and watch him closely," she said as they entered the security checkpoint. She twisted to look at him. "Got that?"

He nodded. "I got it. Mason said he's looking for him." He was reading the next text that came in. They'd been steady for the last ten minutes. "He's in position at the demonstration. He's standing at the back door."

"That's nice, but I could be shot from anywhere in the damn room. I'd rather have him beside me."

Hawk picked up the phone and called Mason instead of texting this time. Good. He quickly relayed the message. That made her feel better. Slightly.

Knowing Mason was waiting for her, lifted her heart. She needed to see him again. To be hugged. She'd had such a shitty morning. And after the best night of her life. She leaned her head back and closed her eyes, so hot and puffy now. She kinda blacked out at that point. She had to prepare for what was coming. It was going to be close.

In many ways.

★

MASON REALIZED SHE was safe if she was giving orders like she had been, according to Hawk. He could believe it. He needed to hear the details of the nightmare she'd been put through already and knew it was likely bad, but she was alive and that was what counted. She just needed to do this demonstration. And he was going to stand at her side and make sure she was safe.

Guilt ate at him. He'd hated the orders pulling him away from her. Had been working since finding out she'd been kidnapped on sourcing where the orders had come from. And why. He'd fought leaving her but on the assurance that several other men were going to be there looking after her, he'd gone to make sure she'd be safe after leaving the hotel.

But instead she and Hawk had damn near died. Again.

So much for those assurances. But he was on it. And had his suspicions now. Then again Tesla's father had helped. Hawk had contacted him as soon as he knew.

The conversation still burned his gut. But at least he'd cared. After the first meeting Mason had wondered. This time there'd been no doubt.

"She's been kidnapped? Again?" The panic and incredulity in his voice had gone a long way to helping Hawk understand the man's emotions had been tightly banked before.

But not now. He hadn't wasted time with ripping Mason to pieces. He wanted details. And then gave him a little background on one of the men above Mason.

Check out…

No reason given. Just the name. Followed by, "Find her and bring her back to me."

When Mason had called back to let him know she was on her way home again, her father had gone silent. He'd released an emotional sigh of relief then had immediately turned business-like. "Is she going to the hospital?"

"She's coming for the demonstration. She refuses to do anything less."

"Then I'll be there." And he hung up. He'd sounded like he meant it.

Mason hoped her father made it. For her sake and maybe his. Sounded like there was some healing needed.

That Tesla had been hurt again was something Mason needed time to get over. But she was alive. They could live with everything else.

He shook his head. How many more lives did she have? She was more cat than human at this rate. His communicator squawked. "She's entering the side door."

Mason raced to the door to be able to open it for her. He was attracting attention, and he didn't give a damn.

The door opened and Hawk grabbed him, shoving him back a few steps and out of the doorway. "Mason. Man, you need to hold back when you see her."

"Why?" That was a hell of thing to say. He glared at Hawk. "You look like shit."

"She's been beaten. And she's got cracked ribs. And she's looking...a little rough."

Mason's fists clenched as he realized what Hawk was saying. "You said she's okay?"

"She is. In fact, she says she's fine." He paused and rolled his eyes. "And she's a hell of a liar too. I know the ribs are cracked as I checked them myself. Her eyes are almost swollen shut and the wind coming back made them worse."

Her eyes and ribs. He got it.

"Those bastards are dead." He turned, looking for Tesla, and caught sight of someone standing hesitantly, her back to him, in front of the entrance. Her long sweater had stretched well past her hips. Only it was ripped and bloody – just like her jeans. As he got closer he could see her fingernails were bloody and torn. She turned to face him.

His fists clenched.

His gut heaved.

His heart died a little.

It was Tesla. And she'd been not just beat up. She'd been *beaten*.

God he was going to kill the bastard behind this.

Just then the announcer said, "Now let me introduce the creator of this program. Miss Tesla Landers."

There was a lot of murmuring going on behind him, but he was staring at Tesla, wondering what she was going to do. Then he realized what the problem was. When introduced, she'd turned and walked several feet forward to the base of the stairs leading to the podium. And stopped. She was looking at the stairs, but she was having trouble seeing them. Her depth perception was off. And she wasn't sure what to do.

Meaning she hadn't seen him.

He strode to her side, and in a calm movement, reached for her hands and held her swollen fingers in his gentle grasp. "Let me help you."

She gasped with joy and clutched at him. He smiled and held her close. "I'm so sorry," he whispered, knowing they had no time.

The gurgle of laughter bubbled up from her chest. "Good," she said. "You can make it up to me later."

He grinned. After all she'd been through... But she was right.

This was not the time. "The stairs are right in front of you," he said.

She nodded. "Oh thank God you're here. I'm so scared," she whispered as he helped her up the stairs.

"You, after being shot at, beaten, and survived being thrown out of a helicopter and a drowning. What could possibly scare you?"

He was genuinely puzzled. He'd yet to see anything rattle her. Stuff that would send normal men running had her sucking in her gut and facing the enemy.

"What if they don't like it?" she whispered as they walked the long road across the stage to where the mic waited. Mason knew he'd likely catch hell for being on the stage with her, but there was no way he was going to desert her right now. He was also shielding her from the curious eyes staring at them. They'd see her soon. That would cause a hell of a reaction.

He heard Hawk's voice on the communicator. Calm, dependable, powerful Hawk. Giving orders and moving into position as if he'd just woken up from a nap.

The table stood in front of them. "You don't have to do this," he whispered, his voice caught by the mic and reaching out across the room. He winced.

The audience shuffled uneasily.

"I'm fine," she said.

In a voice that reached to the back of the room, Tesla repeated, "Against all odds, I'm fine." Then she patted his arm, told him to stay close and stepped around him to face the audience.

A CRESCENDO OF cries filled the air. The announcer rolled over to her. She held up her hand to stop him. "Good morning. Some of you know that I am Tesla Landers. Some of you met me last night where I gave a presentation of my work. This morning I'm giving a demonstration of how it works and what it can do. However, most of you have no idea what I've been through to get here. What others have done to try and stop me. And to gain my work for their own use. So let me tell you."

In clear details, some Mason hadn't even heard yet, she stood tall and calmly told the massive audience sitting rapt all the details of what had happened this last week.

Instead of appearing terrified, she was steady and convincing as hell. When she came to the part about Hawk and fearing he was dead, Mason could feel the color bleaching from his own skin. Lord what she'd been through...

"Now let me tell you why I'm sharing all this..."

The audience was silent... "It's because what I have created *will* save lives. Our soldiers, men and women who stand for us each and every day – *their* lives. For the lives of the men who have saved me every time this last week. I know SEALs aren't supposed to get the glory but these men..." she pointed to Hawk in the back of the room, Swede on the far side, Cooper in the front, and Dane against the left wall and Shadow, standing in the shadows on the right. Her final gesture was to turn and motion to Mason himself. "I have nothing of value to give them in thanks but to see that this program does what it's intended to do. Save *their* lives that they might in turn help someone else in need."

"So how does it work?" She turned on the projector. With all eyes on her, she lifted her necklace over her head and unhooked the cross she had dangling on the end. With a simple motion she proceeded to pop it into two pieces and plug one side into her laptop.

Shit. She'd been wearing that thing the whole damn time. Mason's shocked gaze went from one of his men to the other and saw the same shock in each of their faces. No one had guessed. She'd been wearing that necklace the whole time she'd been captive in enemy hands – and they never knew. He caught sight of his commanding officer and saw the same surprise on his face. But his second in command at his side…yeah, that wasn't a look he'd ever expected to see.

And damn if Tesla's father hadn't called it. He lifted his communicator and said to Hawk, "Dodgson is looking ready to make a move."

"Swede is already on it. He saw the same damn look."

Swede reached the man in seconds, who only at the last moment realized the threat bearing down on him. The man jumped up and bolted to the door. Hawk stepped in front of him, his fist connecting with the man's jaw.

The officer dropped like a stone to the floor. Hawk and Swede bent and lifted him and whisked him away, their actions only causing a small disturbance in the room. All eyes were on Tesla and her program as she led them through the process of what it could do and what her future plans for the program were going to be.

When she finished, she fell silent for a long moment. Then she said, "I lost my brother to the job. He knew I was working on this. For him, I finished it." She gave a tremulous smile. "I've called it Harry's Hope."

She straightened and looked around the room. "Are there any questions?"

And the place erupted.

In a calm orderly fashion, she stood until she looked like she couldn't stand any longer, and answered the questions as they were fired at her.

Finally, the room fell silent.

Mason stepped up and offered his arm.

She accepted. "Ladies and Gentlemen, if there are no more questions, I'm sure you'll understand if I leave you now to think about this while I go find a doctor to check out my broken ribs," she said in a dry, humorous voice and she withdrew her USB and clicked it back into a cross. As she replaced the piece on her necklace, she added, "And as long as Mason's taking me, I know I'll get there safe."

The audience chuckled.

Then she added, "Except if we're going on a helicopter. Then I'm going with Hawk."

And she turned and walked away. The audience stood and clapped as she left. She lifted a hand in acknowledgment and kept walking.

Mason had never been more proud of anyone in his life.

She was something.

And what she was – was his.

She just didn't know it yet.

CHAPTER 27

"NOW IF WE can keep you safe and out of trouble long enough to heal..." The nurse smiled down at her. "You just need to stay in bed for a couple of days and let your body get over this trauma."

She nodded and curled up under the sheets. She really hated hospitals. Although this was a nicer one than most. "I could go home and sleep."

"Maybe. Waiting on the rest of those X-rays first. If the doctor is good with them, then you can. But you have to rest. No more racing around the countryside."

"My racing days are done," she whispered, yawning.

"Good. Sleep a bit. When you wake up the doctor will be here."

She barely heard the rest of the nurse's statement as the warmth and coziness of being curled up in bed, all the nastiness of the last few days over and the stress of the presentation and demonstration gone, finally allowed her to relax.

Destress. Not that she knew what that was. Still, she needed downtime in a big way. Talk about surviving a week of hell.

Mason had helped her off the stage, and she was ashamed to admit she'd all but collapsed on him afterwards. But he took it in stride, picking her up and rushing her here. She hadn't seen him since.

In fact, outside of the nurse she hadn't seen anyone.

She wasn't sure what was to happen next. Was her little house she'd been in prior to the latest kidnapping available to return to? Did she want to go back there? She was of mixed feelings over that. She'd loved Mason there but had been kidnapped as well. Not exactly a good balance. Later, she'd think of it later.

She also felt naked, until she reached up and clasped her necklace. She'd loved the start of surprise from the audience when she'd unclicked it and hooked up the special USB end on it. The enemy had to be kicking themselves over that. She'd been asked to come back in a few days for a more in-depth session. Of course she'd been pleased to accept.

But she wouldn't be showing them everything until she had a contract. She had a long list of add-ons she wanted to develop. She had to decide on a priority list first. And hire more help. She frowned, her fingers pleating the sheets.

Poor Robert. He hadn't survived. His body had been found, dumped in the woods by his house.

The whole scenario felt…odd now. There'd been so much tension, fear…just that unknowing had driven her for so long she felt cut off. At loose ends in a way. As if adrift and no idea of what to do or how to do it.

Maybe that was okay too.

She closed her eyes and drifted. There were sounds in the hallway. Doctors talking. Clipped footsteps. Her room was empty and there were birds chirping outside yet everything was muted. She yawned again and snuggled deeper.

Sleep waited just outside of her awareness. But she couldn't seem to get there. She needed sleep.

Sinking deeper she reached for it.

And slept.

She barely felt the needle go into her arm. Or the sheets under her lifting as she was moved to another bed. As the awareness of something happening to her filtered into her subconscious, she struck out, her arms falling limply at her side. The cold hit her next as she was suddenly outside. Then inside a vehicle. She struggled to open her eyes, but there was a weird set of colors everywhere. She had no idea what the heck was going on.

"Mason," she cried, only her voice was weak as a kitten.

She collapsed back to the bed, and the last thing she heard was someone saying, "She's out. Finally."

"Good, the plane is ready. Let's get the hell out of this damn country."

HAWK HEARD THE rustling beside him. They weren't in rooms yet just in the small examining rooms. His head was booming like a series of rockets going off.

Mason walked in. "Hey. What are you still doing in bed?"

"Trying to get this asshole in my head to stop trying to break his way out." He waved to the space around them. "This is hardly even a room. You can hear everything. It's making my head boom like rockets going off."

"You're off duty until that's fixed."

"Good luck with that. Loved the nurse, I overheard her say something to Tesla about no more running around and she needed to rest."

"Yeah, like that girl needs the reminder."

"I know." Hawk grinned. "She's good people."

Mason nodded, staring at the curtain that surrounded Tesla. He'd tried to see her earlier, but the nurse had kept him away. Only now there appeared to be several people in there. And why was that?

"The doctors maybe?" Hawk suggested in a low voice, but he didn't sound like he believed it himself. Mason slid to the curtain and peered around the corner. Two men dressed as orderlies were moving her to another bed, only she didn't seem pleased to go. Was she hitting them? Damn. The men pushed the bed to the door and maneuvered it out into the hallway.

He watched a moment longer until the man whose back was facing him, turned slightly. Just enough that he could see his profile.

Daniel.

He spun and stared at Hawk, who'd already bolted to his feet. They raced down the hall in the direction the gurney had driven.

By the time they found them again, the orderlies had pushed Tesla down the far end of a hallway and turned the corner. With a shout, they raced after her, catching sight of them again as they barreled out to the loading bay – in time to see Tesla loaded into the back of a waiting ambulance and the men jumping into the front.

"Stop," Mason roared as the doors slammed shut. He sprinted to the vehicle only to have it rip out of the parking lot just as he tried to jump onto the back.

"God damn it," Mason was already calling in the license plate when a jeep came screaming around the corner.

Swede pulled up in front, they hopped in and he took off

after the ambulance.

"Why didn't you take them out at the hospital?" Swede asked.

"Guns in a hospital are never a good thing," Hawk said, his phone ringing.

"And this has to stop once and for all," Mason snapped. "If they are meeting someone then we need to finish this."

He snatched up his phone and listened to an update on the situation. A small plane had caught the radar this morning out in the old airstrip primarily used now for pilot training. A team were there now. The plane had landed last night and was lined up with several other private planes. The other planes were registered and owners were local. Not this one. According to the recent intel, there was no pilot and the plane was just parked.

He relayed the information to the others.

"And if that's not the way these guys are going?"

"Then we take them out sooner than later," Mason snapped.

"Not to worry, look…" he pointed as the ambulance turned down Sexsmith Road, which was the old highway.

"Right direction but it's going to be obvious if we follow," Hawk said.

"No. We can take the shortcut from Taylor Ave and come out ahead of them."

"And take a chance of losing them?" Hawk asked. "We need eyes in the sky on them."

"Already in progress. Should be overhead in a couple of minutes." In fact, he could hear the sounds of a helicopter approaching from the left.

"Isn't an ambulance a little too visible for a getaway vehicle?"

"Oh hell. That's right, they are doing practice rescues at the airstrip today. EMT drills. The ambulance is going to fit right in."

Shit. Mason watched as several other ambulances took the turnoff heading in the same direction. That was three now. Damn it.

The helicopter quickly relayed all were heading to the same location. Without needing to hide any longer, the men moved up between the second and third ambulance. And using the helicopter, kept an eye on the first one.

The convoy hit the old airstrip in ten minutes. The ambulances lined up on the side with the people exiting and gathering around. Mason had no idea what the training schedule was for the EMTs, but he knew Tesla wasn't supposed to be part of it.

Swede drove to the far side of the planes. They quickly disembarked and raced to the plane.

His communicator crackled. "Someone is boarding."

His men moved into position. Mason, hidden behind the wheel on the far side watched as Tesla was picked up and carried to the small set of stairs.

There's no way he was letting that plane take off.

A hawk's cry rent the air. The man carrying Tesla raced toward the stairs and was up in a flash. The third man stopped and turned. Daniel.

Mason stood up. "Hello, Daniel."

Daniel made a startled movement then turned to face him, his hands in his pockets, casual like. "Well, Mason. We meet again."

Mason walked over. "You're not leaving with her, Daniel."

"I am," Daniel said in a conversational tone. "Not sure why you care though."

"Why do you?" Mason snapped. "She already handed over the software."

"Ah, but she's the brains behind it and some of her other ideas now... That's what the buyer is interested in."

"Not happening."

Daniel tilted his arm and shot through his jacket pocket. Just a single pop. Mason had already moved. He came in low and hard and had Daniel on the ground in seconds. With his knee on the gun and his thumb digging into Daniel's neck, he whispered, "You should have chosen someone else, Daniel."

Gasping for air, Daniel asked, "Why?"

He shoved his face into Daniel's. "She's one of us now."

"Like hell."

Hawk stood behind Mason. "He's right."

"She's not a damn SEAL. No way she'd make it."

Mason smiled gently. "I bet that rubs, doesn't it? See, she has something you will never have."

"Loyalty," Hawk said.

"Courage," Dane piped up behind him, pushing the pilot and third man, now cuffed ahead of him.

"Endurance," Swede offered, carrying Tesla in his arms over to the group.

"Determination," Cooper said, walking around from the other side of the plane.

"Grit," said Shadow.

"And on top of all of those, she's got heart," Mason admitted. "And a lot of it. She's SEAL through and through."

"She's nothing but a damn woman," Daniel snapped in an ugly tone. "They are good for one thing and one thing only."

"Oh, programming software to save lives?" Mason asked in a

mocking voice. "Well, you'll get a lot of time to think about how she beat you out in all those categories too because you're going away for a long time."

"I'm going nowhere." Daniel lunged upward and slid a knife out toward Mason.

The single bullet went through his forehead and blew out the back of his brain.

Silence reigned.

Mason spun around to see Swede, a shocked look on his face stare down at the woman in his arms. And his gun that she'd snatched from his shoulder holster was still pointed at the fallen man.

"Jesus, Tesla." Mason raced to her side.

She held the gun up for Swede to put away, and whispered, "If we wipe my prints off, no one will know I did that, right?"

Swede cast a long look in her direction then another around at the dozen or so people converging on them and shook his head. "You could try that line. Not sure it's going to work though."

"Damn."

Mason stood in front of her and glared. He couldn't believe what he'd just heard. And she had the nerve to lift her nose into the air and cling to Swede's arm.

As if he'd protect her from Mason's wrath.

"Do you ever do the expected," he exclaimed.

"What? I was supposed to let him kill you? Besides, Swede's arms were a little busy," she snapped. Her face turned crafty. "Basically, we could just say he used me to shoot Daniel."

"Whoa, leave me out of it," Swede protested.

Mason groaned. He turned away and ran his fingers through

his hair as he stared at the rest of the team now surrounding them. They all wore big grins.

"It's definitely time," Hawk said, smirking.

"Time for what?"

"Time to tell us if you're keeping her," Swede said from behind him. "Cause if you aren't then I am."

"Hell no, I am," Hawk snarled.

Cooper spoke up behind them. "Uhm, if we're placing bids…"

"No. This field is closed." Hawk shook his head at his old friend. "And you were too damn late."

"It's too damn late for all of you," snarled Mason, his voicing thundering as he added, "I'm keeping her."

Silence.

And he turned around, a frown on his livid face. "Now if only she'd stop going missing!"

CHAPTER 28

TESLA STARED AT Mason, the several comments she'd barely caught now blasting back into her memory. They were talking about him and how he felt about her. She didn't know what to say. Everyone stared at her. Everyone waited for her.

For what?

To tell him she was happy to be kept. Hell no, she wasn't. But she was happy to know he wanted to keep her.

It would be nicer if he wasn't glaring at her like he'd rather have his teeth pulled out one by one rather than have such a discussion. Then again, she had to admit she wasn't the most open about such things either.

And she hadn't expected to have this discussion out in the open and surrounded as they were.

Swede gave her a half shake, reminding her she was still in his arms. "Well?"

She ignored his question, her mind consumed with Mason's outburst. When he shook her again, she had to wonder why he was still holding her? Right. Drugs. She wasn't able to stand. Or was she?

With Swede's help, she slowly lowered herself to her feet and rested there for a moment. Happy to feel her feet hold her stable, but still hanging onto Swede, she took the few steps to Mason's side and said, "You might *want* to keep me, but you've done a piss poor job of doing so up to now."

The others cracked up.

Mason stared her, guilt written all over his face. "I know. I'm so damn sorry."

"That's okay. You have the rest of our lives to make up for it."

And she wrapped her arms around his neck and kissed him. Like, she laid it on him. When she released him and he wavered slightly, still grasping for balance, she turned to the others. "Just so we know who's going to be keeping who."

The group rushed forward, and laughing.

Mason reached through the crowd and said in a dark silky voice, "If you're going to kiss me, you'd better do it right."

And he tugged her gently back into his arms and kissed her long, hard and sinfully deep – while the others cheered. The waves of noise rolled over her head, but she was blind to everything but Mason. His love and joy and heat, and the response coiling inside of her.

God she loved this man.

She felt him start and realized she'd whispered that against his lips.

"Love you back, Tesla," he murmured and crushed his lips to hers.

When he lifted his head, a smile of male satisfaction surfing his lips, he looked down at her sagging in his arms and whispered, "We can keep this up for a long time, or...we can go back to your place, after all you need to rest and heal, and we can take this to the next level in private."

She smiled up at him. "Now that's the best idea I've heard all day."

This concludes Book 1 of SEALs of Honor: Mason.

Book 2 is available.

Hawk: SEALs of Honor, Book 2

Buy this book at your favorite vendor.

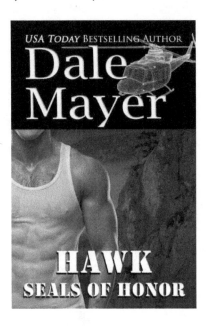

Author's Note

Thank you for reading Mason: SEALs of Honor, Book 1! If you enjoyed the book, please take a moment and leave a short review.

Dear reader,

I love to hear from readers, and you can contact me at my website: www.dalemayer.com or at my Facebook author page. To be informed of new releases and special offers, sign up for my newsletter. And if you are interested in joining my street team, here is the Facebook sign up page.

Cheers,
Dale Mayer

Touched by Death

Adult RS/thriller

Get this book at your favorite vendor.

Death had touched anthropologist Jade Hansen in Haiti once before, costing her an unborn child and perhaps her very sanity.

A year later, determined to face her own issues, she returns to Haiti with a mortuary team to recover the bodies of an American family from a mass grave. Visiting his brother after the quake, independent contractor Dane Carter puts his life on hold to help the sleepy town of Jacmel rebuild. But he finds it hard to like his brother's pregnant wife or her family. He wants to go home, until he meets Jade – and realizes what's missing in his own life. When the mortuary team begins work, it's as if malevolence has been released from the earth. Instead of laying her ghosts to rest, Jade finds herself confronting death and terror again.

And the man who unexpectedly awakens her heart – is right in the middle of it all.

By Death Series

Touched by Death – Part 1 – FREE
Touched by Death – Part 2
Touched by Death – Parts 1&2
Haunted by Death
Chilled by Death

Vampire in Denial

This is book 1 of the Family Blood Ties Saga

Get this book at your favorite vendor.

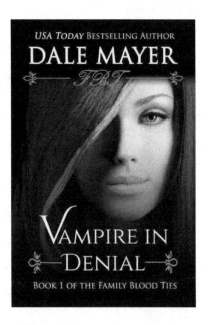

Blood doesn't just make her who she is...it also makes her what she is.

Like being a sixteen-year-old vampire isn't hard enough, Tessa's throwback human genes make her an outcast among her relatives. But try as she might, she can't get a handle on the vampire lifestyle and all the...blood.

Turning her back on the vamp world, she embraces the human teenage lifestyle—high school, peer pressure and finding a boyfriend. Jared manages to stir something in her blood. He's smart and fun and oh, so cute. But Tessa's dream of a having the perfect boyfriend turns into a nightmare when vampires attack the movie theatre and kidnap her date.

Once again, Tessa finds herself torn between the human world and the vampire one. Will blood own out? Can she make peace with who she is as well as what?

Warning: This book ends with a cliffhanger! Book 2 picks up where this book ends.

Family Blood Ties Series

Broken Protocols

Get this book at your favorite vendor.

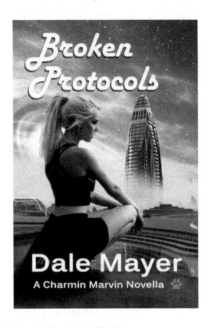

Dani's been through a year of hell...

Just as it's getting better, she's tossed forward through time with her orange Persian cat, Charmin Marvin, clutched in her arms. They're dropped into a few centuries into the future. There's nothing she can do to stop it, and it's impossible to go back.

And then it gets worse...

A year of government regulation is easing, and Levi Blackburn is feeling back in control. If he can keep his reckless brother in check, everything will be perfect. But while he's been protecting Milo from the government, Milo's been busy working on a present for him...

The present is Dani, only she comes with a snarky cat who suddenly starts talking...and doesn't know when to shut up.

In an age where breaking protocols have severe consequences, things go wrong, putting them all in danger...

Charmin Marvin Romantic Comedy Series

Broken Protocols

Broken Protocols 2

Broken Protocols 3

Broken Protocols 3.5

Broken Protocols 1-3

About the Author

Dale Mayer is a USA Today bestselling author best known for her Psychic Visions and Family Blood Ties series. Her contemporary romances are raw and full of passion and emotion (Second Chances, SKIN), her thrillers will keep you guessing (By Death series), and her romantic comedies will keep you giggling (It's a Dog's Life and Charmin Marvin Romantic Comedy series).

She honors the stories that come to her – and some of them are crazy and break all the rules and cross multiple genres!

To go with her fiction, she also writes nonfiction in many different fields with books available on resume writing, companion gardening and the US mortgage system. She has recently published her Career Essentials Series. All her books are available in print and ebook format.

Connect with Dale Mayer Online

Dale's Website – www.dalemayer.com
Twitter – @DaleMayer
Facebook – facebook.com/DaleMayer.author

Also by Dale Mayer

Published Adult Books:

Psychic Vision Series

Tuesday's Child – FREE

Hide'n Go Seek

Maddy's Floor

Garden of Sorrow

Knock, Knock…

Rare Find

Eyes to the Soul

Now You See Her

Psychic Visions 3in1

By Death Series

Touched by Death – Part 1 – FREE

Touched by Death – Part 2

Touched by Death – Parts 1&2

Haunted by Death

Chilled by Death

Second Chances...at Love Series

Second Chances – Part 1 – FREE

Second Chances – Part 2

Second Chances – complete book (Parts 1 & 2)

Charmin Marvin Romantic Comedy Series

Broken Protocols

Broken Protocols 2

Broken Protocols 3

Broken Protocols 3.5

Broken Protocols 1-3

Broken and... Mending

Skin

Scars

Scales (of Justice)

Glory

Genesis

Tori

Celeste

Biker Blues

Biker Blues: Morgan, Part 1

Biker Blues: Morgan, Part 2

Biker Blues: Morgan, Part 3

SEALs of Honor

Mason: SEALs of Honor, Book 1

Hawk: SEALs of Honor, Book 2

Dane: SEALs of Honor, Book 3

Swede: SEALs of Honor, Book 4

Shadow: SEALs of Honor, Book 5

Cooper: SEALs of Honor, Book 6

Collections

Dare to Be You…

Dare to Love…

Dare to be Strong…

RomanceX3

Standalone Novellas

It's a Dog's Life

Riana's Revenge

Published Young Adult Books:

Family Blood Ties Series

Vampire in Denial – FREE

Vampire in Distress

Vampire in Design

Vampire in Deceit

Vampire in Defiance

Vampire in Conflict

Vampire in Chaos

Vampire in Crisis

Vampire in Control

Family Blood Ties 3in1

Sian's Solution – A Family Blood Ties Short Story

Design series

Dangerous Designs – FREE

Deadly Designs

Darkest Designs

Design Series Trilogy

Standalone

In Cassie's Corner

Gem Stone (a Gemma Stone Mystery)

Time Thieves

Published Non-Fiction Books:

Career Essentials

Career Essentials: The Résumé

Career Essentials: The Cover Letter

Career Essentials: The Interview

Career Essentials: 3 in 1

CPSIA information can be obtained
at www.ICGtesting.com
Printed in the USA
BVHW041046141119
563827BV00013B/241/P